Sal Raniero's
little
black
book 1

kailee reese samuels

Sal Raniero's Little Black Book 1
The Phoenix Journals Vol. 1
Copyright © 2020 by Kailee Reese Samuels

All rights reserved. No part of this book may be reproduced or transmitted in any form or by any means, electronic or mechanical, including, but not limited to, photocopying or by any information storage and retrieval system, without permission in writing from the author, except in the case of author credited, brief quotations in reviews.

This is a work of fiction. The names, characters, places, and incidents are products of the writer's imagination or have been used fictitiously and are not to be construed as real. Any resemblance to persons living or dead, actual events, locale, or organizations is entirely and purely coincidental.

All characters depicted in sexual acts in this work of fiction are 18 years of age or older.

First Print Edition: January 16, 2020
ISBN 978-1-947362-86-4

Editing by The Red Pen Queen

BOOKS BY KAILEE REESE SAMUELS

a Tomb of Ashen Tears Books

Salt Kissed Love

Famous Last Words

Every Minute I Love You

Diary of a Submissive

A Dark Place

Forbidden Sins

Talking With Ghosts - *pre-order*

Standalones

the other side of unhappy

Beautiful Things Evil People Do

Chasing Storms

22

A&E

Bad Girl

Madness

Poppy

She/He

SONS

Son of Saint

Son of Angel

Son of Cirque

Sal Raniero Thrillers

Unspoken (Prequel to Hey Pretty)

Sal Raniero's Little Black Book

Prequel (The Contract)

Sal Raniero's Little Black Book 1

The Story of Salvatore

The Initiation

Tea for Two

Grunt

Hopechest

RIDE

Fluff

Bounce

Raw

The JULIET Collection

Juliet

Kinky Sex Magic

Nocturne

A Shimmering Dream

The Red Shoes

Music playlists available on Spotify

PRINTABLE READING LIST - Sal's Reading List

order signed paperbacks from my store
KaileeReeseSamuels.com

WARNINGS
are like cups of tea.

This warning is here for a reason.
This book is a work of fiction containing explicit,
graphic, and violent material.
If you're not 18+, put it the *fuck* down.

Please practice safe sex.
Safe, Sane, and Consensual (SSC) and
Risk-Awareness Consensual Kink (RACK)
practices in BDSM.

Communication is key and I do not believe anything
—sexuality, gender orientation, race, age, or religion
—should be swept under the rug.
If I help stir the cauldron of conversation and
provide an escape for a few hours, I have done
my job.

Don't be afraid to take an emotional breather.

Play hard and have fun.
Be good and love one another.
Enjoy the ride!

Without further ado, here we go…

*To the catty women who told me a girl couldn't write
because of certain 'feminine expectations'
and to the raging bitches who cried out,
"You fucking must!"*

My words are yours.

CONTENTS

Preface xiii

1. Sweet Like Cream 1
2. A Cool Grand 23
3. The River 41
4. The Pulse of Feast or Famine 63
5. People Need People 83
6. Hold My Hand 99
7. Help Me 119

Client #2 141

PREFACE

In the middle of nowhere, Texas, Sugargrove blooms with a picture-perfect quaintness. The small-town atmosphere is built entirely around the BDSM school, Juliet.

The academy is owned solely by Anna Ford.

She wanted to offer submissive a safe place to explore their desires. Initially financed through Anna's mob associations, the criminal underworld still lingers in the sanctuary of Juliet, though it is very hush hush.

~ MAIN RECURRING CAST ~
(More will be added *after* each book releases…)

Anna Ford

The beautiful, older headmistress of Juliet and former Vegas showgirl entertained The Suits —*mafioso*. She had a longterm love affair with Sal's Old Poppa (grandfather), Luca Raniero and offers a safe harbor for the young Sal. In 2008, he does not know the extent of their involvement.

Charlotte Tuddle

A fifteen-year-old resident of Sugargrove and best female friend and fascination of Sal. She lives with her aunt, Ella Hemsworth, who is on the board of directors at Juliet.

Jack Kerris

Gifted plastics surgeon by day and skilled Master at night, Jack understands the opportunity of *The Contract* handed to Sal. Still, his motivations aren't necessarily honest. Conniving and controlling, he will seize any chance to escalate his self-worth, including feigning relationships and alignments in Sugargrove.

Kate Capri

Sal's Mistress, for show only, as an effort to keep the vultures at bay. She maintains a board position at Juliet as a Dominant but is an emotional wreck dealing with her own Maestro's death.

Nico "Nicky" Cristos

After stalking the Raniero family for years, Nico befriended Sal and encouraged his safe passage to Texas. His father, Delarte Cristos, is a shipping magnate, and Nico and Sal find common ground in not wanting anything to do with their family legacies. A deviant sociopath, Nico loves a good pair of shoes on a treacherous, evil woman.

Sal Raniero

Eighteen-years-old and running away from a future with his mafia family, Sal understands both sides of the coin. Nico suggests taking shelter at Juliet as someone else deceptively lures his attention to Texas. While he seeking refuge, this unknown entity keeps eyes on the Dark Prince of the Boston mafia.

After several weeks under Anna's wing in 2008, he signs *The Contract* to become a male escort for her select group of clientele. Attempting to stay under the radar of his tyrannical father, he ends up learning to hustle with a fierce social game relying on loyalty and trust. His good looks and mischievous charm quickly earn him a place in the heart of Sugargrove and his *Little Black Book* clients.

Reflectively in the current day, any references made to *his girl* or *his boy* during his *notes* should be assumed to be Sal's current lovers, Iris Nakamura and Deacon Cruz.

1

SWEET LIKE CREAM

"You're the one-night fantasy, Sal," Charlotte randomly announced, licking her strawberry ice cream cone and making me wish she was about five years older. Three would've done because I refused to play with jailbait. Flirting. Movies. Ice cream dripping on her...*ya, we're friends*. "Stop worrying about what you think you should be. Just give them what you are."

Charlotte Tuddle was the only one I told about *the contract*. Why I chose to tell her was even a mystery to me. I trusted her because there was something about the girl that struck me. We were like long lost kindred spirits.

I figured someone needed to know I was about to go jump in the sack with a random stranger and telling Nicky I was reducing myself to manwhore felt strangely humiliating.

I was the son of the Boston mob boss.

I didn't need the money or attention. Finding a girl for a blow job or a roll in the hay had never been a problem, so why was I doing this?

Though I couldn't admit the answer out loud, I knew.

Intimacy.

I believed the clients were looking for something more than a live-action sex toy. My best guess was they wanted someone to listen to their daily rants about bad children and worse husbands.

Frankly, anything to keep my mind off the future I didn't want with my father was a winner in my book. I wouldn't have to think about the things I knew, the deals he made, the bodies he buried if I was proverbially balls deep in some woman's strife.

I signed the contract to save my soul from absolute damnation.

My dick getting loved on was just the cherry on top.

But it was *never* about that.

If I could distract my mind, I could work the problems out. Otherwise, I would pace the floor, pull my hair, and crack my knuckles. I had been this way for years. Stressed for an algebra test? Go for a run. Needing to write a paper? Go make fresh raviolis with Nonna. Big soccer game? Dive into the latest smut.

Whatever I needed to do, I didn't want to think about it.

For me, overthinking equaled dynamic meltdown and subsequent failure.

Charlotte's tongue eased around the cream, and I glanced away. I couldn't succumb to the whimsical merriment of knowing what that mouth could one day do. It wasn't outlandish, and I wasn't some sort of perv.

She was fifteen; I was eighteen.

The attraction was normal and dare I say, *very real*. It wasn't an uncommon occurrence in the last few weeks to find Charlotte and me together. We were two peas in a pod. Or two kids quietly fondling one another in Anna's swimming pool.

"Do you have any idea how much they're paying for you?"

"Not a fucking clue," I mumbled, not really caring about the earnings of my dick service. I was young and these things—they didn't matter much.

. . .

In many ways, they still don't. I'll forever be a slave striving for the connection and the memories more than the cold hard cash. I genuinely wanted to get to know my clients, fucking them was the least of my concern because I could fuck anyone. It wasn't rocket science.

Watching a couple of kids swinging and chasing one another, I took a swig of my quad shot caramel macchiato and lit a smoke. Charlotte stuck her ice cream in front of my mouth.

"Taste it!"

"You just want to play swapsies as an excuse to drink all my coffee."

With her blonde hair gleaming in the sun, she grinned with an innocence. "You love me!"

As much as I hated to admit that, she was right. Not in a romantic way, but in a, if one of her many male admirers messed with her, I'd kill them kind of way. It wasn't like I didn't know how to street brawl or maim a body, but those weren't the primary tools in my box. I liked to talk shit through until a fist-pounding was the only means of getting my point across.

"What if this is a giant mistake?"

"It's not," she assured, biting into the cone with

a loud crunch. "If I were in your shoes, I'd jump at the opportunity."

I bent and put my elbows to my knees as I glared at her over the top rim of my sunglasses. I was flabbergasted. "… You'd be a call girl?"

"I said *if* I was in your shoes. That implies I'd have a dick."

"But you wouldn't do it as a female?"

She curled her legs up under her bottom. "Not unless the clientele was stable. Too much risk."

Strange thing was, I knew she was right about that too. There was a big difference between going to entertain some horny MILF as opposed to Charlotte being some old geezer's sugar baby. The laws of sexual promiscuity were not equal.

Good thing they didn't need to be.

Especially in terms of Charlotte.

"I have to meet with this guy on Sunday night, too." I stared at the text message with the address. "I agreed to humor his fetish."

With her sticky fingers, she swiped the phone from my hand and stared at the screen. "Sal, do you know where this is?"

I shrugged, not having a clue. I knew where Kate's house was and where Juliet was and the route between the two down Main Street. I hadn't looked around much because Anna wanted me laying low.

I was her comeback.

The Grande Dame of the BDSM school, Anna Ford, didn't say it, but I knew. The economic climate of 2008 forced a lot of changes, and by our conversations, I understood Juliet had taken a blow too. The old money members were as active as ever, but getting the new, young crowd—they weren't blowing money out their ass on exclusive memberships to a sex club either.

Anna was grooming me for when everyone finally came out of their shell. I'd be poised and the prime grade-A cut of man meat she needed to flip the narrative and get her beloved school back on top.

I was...*excited* about the prospect.

Mostly because I wanted to help Anna. My loyalty was nothing less than determined to help her succeed. If she wanted my assistance, I'd help her, because she opened her door despite knowing the violence that I could bring. I was the son of a mafia lord.

And things could get messy quickly.

Very messy. Very quickly.

Thankfully, Anna was an expert at dealing with the slop of boys like me.

. . .

I remember this conversation with Charlotte sitting on the park bench like it was yesterday. She never tried to impress me because she knew I wouldn't go there. Dare I say, she was the average All-American girl with hopes and dreams, and somehow, she brought those fundamental values home to my heart.

And that blew me over the damn moon.

No makeup. Truth-filled words. Burps.

The athletic shorts showing off her booty didn't hurt, but the attention I bestowed wasn't about that. Charlotte was real. And when I was young, walking around with the gifts God gave, and everyone was filling my head with how beautiful I was and the future I had waiting for me—all I wanted was someone real.

I didn't want a girl by my side showcasing something she was not.

I needed a girl to breathe real.

I just didn't realize, when I finally found her, she'd be as lethal as me. I didn't know that getting everything I wanted would come at a steep price—she would play the game.

At times, better than me.

Before I digress...Charlotte and I are still friends. Though time plays evil tricks on relationships, if I ever needed someone to just listen without judgement or analysis —Charlotte Tuddle would have my back.

"You need to drive by the address, babe."

"I guess I can," I replied, inhaling on the smoke. "But, I have to leave soon for my weekend with Trudy Diaz."

Her eyes widened. "Oooh…shit!"

"What?"

"She's going to eat you alive," she informed, finishing her ice cream. "And if she doesn't, the Hail Mary's might."

I shot her a glare. "What does that mean?"

"That address is for the Catholic church."

Slumping back into the bench, I covered my face with my hands. "I signed a deal to be the priest's whipping boy…"

"Father Quinn isn't bad, but you need to be damn careful."

The few white clouds drifted in the blue sky as I understood her words loud and clear and fathomed a guess, "He's mob."

"I don't know that he's necessarily mob, but he's not innocent."

I blinked over to her sweet face and longed to spend the rest of the weekend together. "Do I want to know how you know this?"

"Let's just say Aunt Ella knows how to repent for her sins."

I groaned, "Fuck."

After dropping Charlotte off at the eccentric modern mansion, which was weirdly stark white with vast panes of glass set back in the woods, and belonged to Ella Hemsworth, I took her up on the suggestion and drove by the church. While not as vast as I was accustomed to, the building was bigger than I expected for the town of three thousand, but it wasn't the size of the structure that struck me as off.

The grandiose opulence of it hit when I noted the gas flame lanterns trimmed in gold when I stopped the car in the empty lot.

Getting out, I noted the clear blue skies pregnant with ominous dark clouds. I lit a smoke and wandered closer to the chapel.

The lavish architecture continued as I hiked up the steps to the heavy wooden door. The grain was stained red with gold embellishments and iron fretwork. My inner woodworker was impressed as I laid my hand flat against the door. Immediately, upon stepping inside, I felt a strange premonition like there was something to learn here besides the catechisms.

From the vestibule, I peeked into the cathedral. Stained glass windows lined the upper walls. Behind the altar, an enormous statue of the Virgin Mary waited without judgement or claim. She was a beautiful interpretation, and without a doubt, the source of many a young man's fantasies. If it sounds sacrilegious, it's not. I had long conversations with Nicky in complete dives over greasy hamburgers concerning this very thing.

She's the mother and the Mistress.

The holy and unholy.

Somewhere in all of that, there is balance, forgiveness, and absolution.

Walking to the front pew, I genuflected like the good Catholic I was—*and still am to a certain extent* when I heard the unmistakable Creole voice. "I was just about to lock up." The woman smiled and clasped her hands together. "I will leave you to pray. If you need anything…"

"... Ma'am?" I interrupted as her eyes lit up. Her brows twitched at my heavy Bostonian.

And back then, before immersing into the plains and drawls of Texas, my Boston accent was thick. It's evolved over the years, but when I'm angry, I always sound like a damn daego. With unbreakable roots tying my soul back to the motherland and my hometown, I evoke the blur of my cultural heritage. It is easily discernible.

"Yes?"

"Is Father Quinn here?"

"No, Salvatore," she eagerly replied. "He's up in Arkansas, fishing with some old friends."

Now, there were multiple ways to interpret her statement, and I knew that even then. He was either literally fishing with a pole or fishing out potential associates. I remember quietly snorting because I had bets on the latter. The upstanding priest had a story.

But they all did...

In the back rooms of dirty delis and the alleys of restaurants and between the cans of red ripe tomato sauce and fifty kinds of ugly olives at the market, I was raised to converse in code. So, it didn't seem absurd that the lovely Creole woman with her pretty dark complexion and stark white hair might do the same.

Never underestimate anyone.

"He'll be back late Sunday night and asked that you stop by the rectory on your way home."

"Since you know who I am," I replied with a smirk. "Who are you?"

"I'm Perrine Baptiste, the secretary for the parish in Sugargrove. My assistant, Laverne Romano, will be here Sunday for Deacon Munoz's service."

My system was in overdrive.

I had a presumably white Padre wanting to whip me, his Creole secretary, her very Italian sounding assistant, and a Hispanic priest. This might not seem very important, but in actuality, knowledge of the diversity calmed me. I knew from being around Anna that a good many of her students were international, and she embraced the broader scope of the world.

My father believed solely in Italians.

And he routinely spewed his hatred of everyone else.

Of course, I was an early rebel and brought home my Middle Eastern friend, Bilal Amari, when I was five. I was good at finding such trouble, and Dad practically had a coronary until Mama convinced him that one ethnic friend was alright.

One turned into many...

And I've got scars from those wars.

Perrine seemed to notice my inner reflection, and her maternal sirens cued off with a warning siren as she suggested, "Come have a glass of lemonade."

It was the best fucking glass of lemonade ever.

I can still taste the sweet and tart on my tongue of Perrine's magic nectar she brought forth to heal and comfort. Like so many others, my heart misses her spirit and craves the time like a starved child. And before you ask, she passed less than four years later from cancer.

But God, she was good.

Good like my Nonna. Good like the Virgin Mary. And a damn good introduction into how things were "different" in Louisiana. She taught me how to eat, snapping tails and sucking heads of crawfish, and how to cook. I can make killer étouffée. And somehow that made it all right that I was a kingpin's son on the run. She coated my choices in her pungent, aromatic flavors, and I swallowed every one of them with ease.

There was always great amounts of divine food and conversation with laughter and tears and moments to remember.

On her death bed, she teasingly called herself my "Colored Mama." While I was slightly taken aback by her bluntness, I simply replied, "You were the only Mama that ever mattered."

Because it was true.

I loved my mama, but she had a passivity when it came to my father's hand that I could never forget or forgive. She rarely stood up for her runt of a son and turned the other cheek as he bashed mine in for eighteen years.

Perrine healed me. She fused the gaping hole between my being lost and found and ignited love and passion inside of me. I don't mention her often because…it hurts.

Few things will instantly bring me to my knees, and Perrine remains one of them.

I'd learn in time that the family extended far and wide, and the ass she wiped in a lavish Southern plantation was one day the ass I would love fucking.

In my expensive custom suit and Deacon in his Reckless Rebellion cut and best jeans, we sobbed like orphans the day we lost our Mama. And then we did what she would've wanted—we feasted like Kings without a care in the world.

Since I've brought up my biker boy, Deacon Cruz, he never called his biological mother anything other than Ma, and the reason for that was the Queen of Lemonade, his "Mama"—and yes, even sometimes his "Mamie"—belonged to none other than Perrine Baptiste.

As it would turn out, Father Quinn had significant ties to New Orleans and Victor "Saint" Cruz, Deacon's father. The elder Saint insisted Quinn take the lovely Perrine as his secretary and confidante.

SITTING ON THE BACK DECK OF THE Catholic Church in Sugargrove in the summer of 2008, I confided all my fears and confessed all my sins over lemonade and a half pack of Marlboros. She held my hand, laughed when I laughed and cried when I cried.

Perrine knew who I was going to meet that evening, and her only words of advice regarding Trudy Diaz still hold true to this day. "Hold on tight, boy," she said giggling. "And if she gets rowdy, pull her hair, and show her who is boss."

I was eighteen.

Not only was Gertrude "Trudy" Howser Diaz more than twice my age, but she was Deacon Cruz's mother and the old lady of the President of the Delirium MC.

How I got here, I wasn't sure.

But she was about to make a man out of me.

And Trudy was about to go from MILF to the first of many MIHF—Moms I Have Fucked.

---

message from Hot Mama:
Meet me at Clint Ray's Bar & Grill on Friday at 7 PM. It's just outside of San Antonio. Don't be late.
Don't worry about clothes for the weekend. You won't need them. See you then, Sugar.

WITH THE TOOTHBRUSH IN MY TREMBLING hand, I peered at the message for the thousandth time. I don't know if I expected it to change or have another one pop up. I gurgled a gulp of water in my mouth and spat before wiping the steam from the mirror and staring at my reflection in my room at Anna's house. I wasn't sure about any of this, but I needed to know who these people were and what made them tick.

Lathering up my cheeks, I carefully ran the razor blade over my skin. I was shaking so hard that I was sure I would end up nicked and cut only to arrive with little bits of bloodied tissue paper everywhere. I slowed down and thanked the heavens I hadn't packed the straight razor Old Poppa taught me to use.

Hell, I might not have even made it here.

Accidents happen—people get trapped in their heads and do stupid shit. I wasn't immune.

If that meant kicking back a few beers at a bar and knocking boots with a horny older woman, I was okay with that. I was young, and they were paying. I was going to have a helluva good time while I could because when you're walking around with a dick and your last name is Raniero; time is borrowed, stolen, or lent for only a certain amount of time. When the bill comes due, you pay it or die.

My father was but a guppy in the ocean of hungry sharks, and he paid dearly for his place on the criminal block. For all the things I could point out that he fundamentally fucked up, the one thing I will gratefully attest to—he kept my four sisters and myself standing. If we were in any imminent danger, we never knew. We all knew the threats and risks posed by his selected line of work, but those mundane things like having a multitude of 'Uncles' around, were typical facets of my childhood. I never understood the idea of *not* having people around with multiple bangs cloaked beneath suit coats.

I lived it. I breathed it. I survived it.

And I was infected by it.

It was only a matter of time—this much I knew—before I succumbed to my destiny, all because I enjoyed the game, and somehow, I believed, I could sell it and shake it better than my old man. Perhaps because I had been raised between my paternal grandfather and my maternal grandmother to evoke a confident, charming bravado while shoving a knife (or ice pick) into someone's backside. *"Do it all with a smile, Salvatore."*

And I did.

In the little black book, I wrote her name down, along with essential details of my private investigation. I wasn't about to go in blind.

Trudy Diaz.

Deacon Cruz's mother.

Deacon was the godson of Anna Ford.

And shit was about to get interesting.

Closing my eyes, I remembered Charlotte's words, *"You're the one-night fantasy."* I lowered my head and said a quiet prayer. After making the sign of the cross and kissing my crucifix, I glanced up to see Anna standing behind me.

"You should warn a boy," I scolded, feeling unnerved.

"You're going to be late, sweet one." She smiled, knowingly, and propping her shoulder against the door jamb. "You need to hurry. It's a good hour to Clint Ray's and Friday night traffic is never kind."

"What are you thinking about?"

"How much you look like your grandfather," she candidly whispered. "If I could go back in time, there are many things I would've done differently. Don't waste a second of it, Salvatore."

Blotting aftershave on, I turned to see her tears first hand. "Anna…"

"Don't come any closer or I will rip that towel from your body."

I grinned like her flirtation was the greatest thing ever—which at that point, it probably was. I thoroughly enjoyed humoring anyone older than me. Earning the attention was a challenge, and girls my age or younger—*the Charlotte's of the sea*—were rare finds.

. . .

Little did I know, Anna was only hitting the cusp of my trifling boyish antics. She was the first wave, escalating with a warning churn that a storm was brewing out beyond the horizon in a place I couldn't see or dare imagine.

When I think about it now in retrospect, I am so glad I had those few weeks to cut my teeth with the former showgirl.

With one word or brush of her hand, Anna could evoke a whole host of emotions, send my ass straight to the shower with my dick in my palm. If I had a dollar for every time I painted those shower walls that summer, I'd be a rich motherfucker on cum shots alone.

It was all grooming.

Training. Practice. Repetition.

And teaching her pupil.

"What should I wear?"

"You're going to a bar in Texas known for ribs and brisket, if you wear anything other than ripped jeans and a t-shirt, then you'll be overdressed."

I snickered. "Got to act the part?"

"Precisely," she said, crossing her arms. "When you go to an exclusive club or five-star restaurant, play that role and do it with ease. Chameleon yourself. Let the only standout be you—your flirtatious wit and priceless smile. Wrap the package accordingly."

A light blush rose on my cheeks. "… Literally and figuratively?"

"I won't lie," she muttered. "I wasn't always the safest hostess, but it's a different world now. Make your decisions and have no regrets about those. You'll know when to walk around without an umbrella, but I would damn sure always be prepared to take cover." She winked as our conversation skirted along the edge of prophylactics and appropriate time and place…and *client*. "But in either case, buy lube."

"Already done, Ma'am."

"Good boy," she proudly praised. "You cannot expect the crowd you're serving to be flowing like Niagara Falls. Be equipped—pocket knife, extra cash, mints. And if you get in a bind," she said, handing a credit card with my name on it to me. "Use it."

"You don't have to do this…"

"I do unless you plan on using Daddy's. You're my responsibility now."

I shook my head. "I left his in my bedroom at home."

"This is your home now, Salvatore. I am your

family. If you find trouble, call me. Have an enjoyable time!"

I didn't know what to say, but I understood why she did it. I was a kid, and Anna had taken on a protective, maternal role since day one. She felt an obligation to care for me, having known Old Poppa.

I had no idea how deep their involvement was at this point or that he was the love of her life. I just assumed he was another one of The Suits, not that he was her favorite Suit.

And that mattered.

If I had known about their love affair back then, I don't know that I would have found the freedom I did.

Anna encouraged the spreading of my wings, and when I got burned, she promised to scoop my body from the ashes and set me off again. She let me naturally evolve without interference, and that took a hell of a woman to be able to do such.

I looked at her with eager, anxious eyes and simply said, "Thank you for changing my life."

"You're so very welcome, Kid."

2

A COOL GRAND

Pulling in the over-packed parking lot of Clint Ray's Bar & Grill at 6:59, I took a deep breath and eyed the multitude of big trucks. I parked in the grass as others had done, killed the engine, and wiped my sweaty palms on my jeans. I wasn't intimidated as much as uncertain. These were cowboys and ranchers and bikers. While the women looked like showpieces with poufy hair and more makeup than a showgirl, boots and jeans were the names of the game for the men.

I wasn't from around here.

And the second I opened my mouth or step foot inside, they'd know that. Regardless of how friendly these folks were, never had the lines been so distinctly drawn for me.

There was Texas.

And there was everywhere else.

There were Texans.

And there was everyone else.

And whatever they were drinking, I wanted some of it—at least the rugged boots, ripped up jeans, and four-wheel drive. And the babe might not be bad if she had heart.

Getting out of the Firebird, I lit a smoke. With my elbows propped on the roof, I stared at the glorious view. The place was remote, set on the far outskirts of a dinky ghost town just waiting to get sucked up by San Antonio.

With the scent of sizzling beef filling the air, I listened as laughter and music boomed from the covered back deck. The honky-tonk with good food sparkled like a diamond—*the dive bar on the side of a farm-to-market road surrounded by cotton and cornfields*.

Lazily slipping down the horizon, the sun showed off a spectacle of pinks and yellows behind the farmlands and two-lane highway. The windmill and grain silo offered a perfect picture of Texas as I tried to catch my breath and decide if the Boston mafia kid could assimilate into the rich environment. And it was rich—perhaps not in Benjamin's—but in swirling, plentiful colors that my imagination could've only dreamed.

I'd have to chameleon.

But not tonight.

I had gel in my hair and looked like a young Italian thug. Because I was a young Italian thug, I understood what the bank could bring, but where I was from, it was all routine—give the loan, sell the drugs, bully for the payment, and when they didn't pay, take them out to the yard to show them who was boss. The money didn't matter as much as power. And I knew I could play that game, but I wanted a different board with people I couldn't read. I needed a challenge because I was bored. And bored people typically find trouble, which was exactly what I was doing in Texas. I was stirring my cauldron.

But... These bastards were going to beat my ass unless I could find common ground.

"If you keep looking like that, we may not make it inside." Her body pressed against mine as her hand drifted south of my belt. And I wasn't even donning a dessert-plate sized silver belt buckle. "And that'd be a shame because rumor has it, you know how to dance."

By the mature twang—which was so fucking sweet—in her voice, I gambled, "Ms. Diaz."

Brushing her hand over the front of my jeans, she whispered, "Call me Trudy. Call me Bitch. Or don't call me at all. And that rule applies to very few, Sally boy."

My dick throbbed.

Fuck.

This was going to be fun.

Absolute heaven. Or pure hell.

With my sunglasses on, I grinned from ear-to-ear as she pinned my body to the car. She might as well have started frisking me because I was guilty on all counts.

Stroking my scruff, I considered her for a second before dropping one arm and gripping her hip, pulling her closer to my backside. "If you're going to ride it, then you best hold on."

Pressing her hands to my shoulders, she smiled and kissed my cheek and giggled. I had her. And she had me—or at least my dick, at full attention, as I slowly spun around. "Salvatore Raniero, I have been waiting for you." Without a care, she took my sunglasses off and scanned over my face. "Dear fuck, those eyes. I could die drowning in those fucking eyes."

And this was how I met Trudy Diaz.

My initial assessment of fun—was spot on. She

was aggressive and assertive with a vulnerability. *And a whole lotta challenge.*

In the dictionary, next to the entry for MILF, there should have been a picture of Trudy Diaz because she was a vision from way too many porn-induced nocturnal emissions.

Loads of dark chocolate and blonde locks framed her face. She was more hair than body with a dainty silhouette, and hazy gray eyes that were stolen from ripe fall days heavy with clouds threatening to bring winter with a blast. Comfort and joy oozed from her being. She was holiday decorations on November 1, lazy Sunday mornings with a cup of coffee and a warm blanket, and burning icicles on fingertips that snapped—*don't fuck with my children, or I'll kill you now and worry about where to bury the body later.*

The profile of Gertrude Howser Diaz might be the best I've ever done because post-Trudy, everything skewed. There was life before her, and there was life after her, and the way I uploaded the world around me—changed.

"Does everyone get this kind of welcome?"

"Only the hot young ones." She laughed. "Are you hungry, sweetheart?"

"Would you believe I'm starving?"

"You look like it," she muttered, taking my hand. "Come on, let Ma feed ya before I do naughty things to ya."

"Ya," I agreed, hereby giving consent for her involvement in my life forevermore. It was that simple, and maybe it was my naivety at eighteen, but I instantly trusted this woman with all of me. "Thank you for coming."

We strolled across the parking lot as she clung to my arm in her four-inch black stiletto leather boots and dark jeans embellished with rhinestones. Her belt was a silver chain dangling—*teasing*—dangerously low on the tightly wrapped package I wanted desperately to unwrap. Her long lashes blinked up to me. "Don't thank me for *coming* yet."

I snorted and opened the door to the revelry tucked inside Clint Ray's. She led the way to a corner table in the back as I noted several people acknowledging her presence.

Heaven knows it wasn't me.

I didn't know anyone in Texas at that point, but it was similar to Boston and the Raniero clan. If we walked into one of those old delis in Boston, I would've gotten the same looks of gratitude mixed with fear Trudy was receiving. People respected her position, which, of course, brought my nervousness to the forefront.

No one ever said changing my entire life was going to be easy or enjoyable.

The promise was to show up and be accountable, not float passively by with a cocktail in hand and a snarl on my face. Life was going to hand over grit. Welcoming my resurrection on my hands and knees, I would have done anything to escape my father's wrath.

Was I going to end up out in the lot with her old man owning my face?

She slid into the circular-shaped booth, which easily could've sat seven, and pointed for me to go around to the back wall. I felt like Trudy was my training wheels, and in a way, she was. "What do you want to drink?"

"Water is fine," I replied as she opened the menu.

"Let's try that again, sugar." She gripped my fingertips with her long pink talons, and I bravely peered up. "What do you *want* to drink?"

"Whiskey, straight," I replied, looking her in the eye. "Unless you're drinking beer, in which case, I'll do a bottle of whatever you are having."

"That's better," she complimented with a huge smile. "But next time, whiskey neat, or whiskey with two cubes, or whiskey with water, or two fingers of whiskey." As she coached, I paid attention to every word because clearly, I had a thing or two or twenty-thousand to learn. "But not whiskey, straight. It's confusing and muddy. Straighten it up. Narrow it down. This is what I want."

She wasn't just talking about booze but radiating with confidence in affirming life choices. After all, I would never escape the surname. I was a Raniero, born and bred and expected. But it was that last bit —*expected*—that I often flubbed on in the early days. The fact was I couldn't swagger until I could crawl.

With my eyes radiating trouble, I teased, "… What if I want four fingers?"

She erupted with a laugh and quipped, "That'll lead to fisting, and you should order the whole bottle."

And so, she did.

Since that night, I've been routinely picked on for my fascination with Jim Beam, but I've tasted almost every whiskey imaginable. My love for JB comes from Trudy and reminds me of where I came from and how far I've traveled.

It is non-negotiable.

Trudy loves Jim Beam, Cuervo Gold, Absolut, and MGD. She smokes Virginia Slims Ultra Lights. She likes her pizza cooked to a crisp, takes bleach baths religiously, and loves all holidays. And she guzzles Pepsi and black coffee by the gallon.

The list could go on and on about her preferences. The point is—Trudy knows what she likes and how she likes it—and nothing changes that. Nothing.

She was the perfect spiritual lesson to stabilize my unsteady. And ya, I got—ya—in casual conversation from her too.

I would love to say my elementary class stopped there, but it didn't. After our bottle and two glasses arrived, she ordered four New York strips in well, medium well, medium rare, and rare, along with one loaded baked potato and two salads with blue cheese.

"I don't like chives," I mumbled as she took the lead.

She grinned and told the curvaceous young girl, who was closer to my age than Trudy, "No chives. Extra sour cream."

"Bacon—I like bacon a lot."

"Extra bacon." The waitress winked.

"And I love blue cheese dressing."

"Extra blue cheese. Do you want extra chunks with that?"

"Sure," I replied with a grin. "I love chunky."

The glowing, voluptuous waitress giggled and asked, "Anything else, T?"

"No, babygirl." Trudy's fingers were still latched onto mine as the waitress bounced away with our order in tow. I stared at all that ass packed inside of those jeans every step of the way. "You're gonna be alright, Sally." She smirked, catching me. "You have this. You don't think you do, but trust me, you do."

"I wish I believed that," I replied. "Does *your*...come here?"

"My what? My husband?" She pulled the pack of smokes from her black leather jacket and flung it off. I took it from her hands, the soft leather still warm and fragrant from her body. She smelled like roses and lemons, and everything clean and good. "No. Javi isn't welcome anywhere near here unless he wants a bullet in the back of his skull, but he is off in Florida on a fishing trip."

There was that word again—*fishing—the* source of my father's legitimate business and the code for all things unsavory. I started to feel like this one word was haunting me like a ghost.

I nodded. "Thank you."

"For?"

I shrugged. "Being you."

"I've tried being other people, and that never works out in my favor." Her expression softened as she took a sip of the whiskey and scanned the crowd. "You like Tara?" I furrowed my brow. "The waitress? Is she your type?"

My lips shifted from side-to-side as I debated how to answer the question. "I don't know my *type* yet."

"So, all girls are a hit."

I chuckled. "Ya, you could say that."

"And how do you feel about being here with an older woman?"

"I'm having a good time," I admitted the truth. "But I'll let you know if that changes."

"Fair enough," she said as Tara brought our salads. Mine was soaked in blue cheese, and I beamed with a grin.

There have been times I have driven out of my way just *to have a chicken salad from Clint Ray's Bar & Grill. Their blue cheese remains some of the best I've ever had. Only now, I walk in with nods and handshakes and the occasional, "How you doing, Sally boy?"*

We chitchatted throughout the salad, taking our own sweet time. The kitchen was running behind with the enormous Friday crowd, but it was okay, neither of us was in a hurry. Trudy brought home the notions of enjoying the moment, experiencing it to its fullest, and not letting it disappear early. Perhaps it was maturity or wisdom or a combination of both, but she wanted to soak me up as much as I did her. Sometimes, you click with people, and Trudy Diaz certainly did with me.

When the steaks finally arrived, I relished in the opportunity to lead and cut every bite. "I do not like it well done."

"Neither do I," she admitted. "I'll take it home to the dogs. Try the rare."

I didn't understand how she was so attuned to the fact that the previous eighteen years, I had no choice. Simple things like steaks came as my father ordered them. It wouldn't take long for me to get it—she fought her husband and the club for her son's right to choose everything in life.

Trudy was just as abused as I was, and it was the ultimate source of our spark. We understood one another like no one could unless they had been in that situation. We spoke the same language of apathetic apologies for trivialities and swayed the blows like ducks headed to a murky pond filled with gators.

The rare steak was delicious and cooked to perfection. We quickly consumed all of it, and Trudy ordered another one to go. A light curl tipped up from the corner of her mouth. "You might be hungry later. If nothing else, we can have steak and eggs in the morning."

And on that note, it brought the reality into play —*I was going home with her*. I was going to spend the entire weekend wrapped up in Trudy Diaz. A wave of nausea swirled in my belly. I was going to know what her body felt like writhing against mine. And I was going to smell like her on the drive back to Anna's house.

"Where do you live?"

"I have a house in Houston near the club and one just north of Austin," she informed, understanding the quizzical look on my face, my thought process, and the questions brought on by the unknown. "Or we can go check into a hotel."

"What kind of dogs?"

"Two pit bulls," she said, smiling. "They're angels—Gabriel and Raphael."

I laughed, feeling a tad more at ease. "And they're in Austin, far away from the club?"

"Yes, Sir," she replied, wiping her mouth and rubbing her lips together as I heard the word *Sir* drop from her lips for the first time. It wouldn't be the last. And I'd be lying if I said it didn't make my cock thicken with a pang of ravenous hunger. I didn't quite understand how one little word could mean so much or how to control the effect it had on me. "The pups are mine and cannot stand him. I go up to Austin almost every weekend since my son left. Javi is too busy chasing the club sluts, and I'm way too old to be one."

"Nah," I declared. "You're a gorgeous woman, Trudy."

"Maybe," she said. "But their party scene isn't my thing much anymore, especially since Deacon ran off."

"When did he leave?"

"He left at sixteen and was arrested at nineteen

on some trumped-up charges. He was just released, and I asked an old friend in New Orleans to look after him."

"How old is he?"

"Christmas baby, 1987. Twenty."

Interestingly enough, while I was busy flirting with Deacon's Ma in Texas, he was off in New Orleans, working his dirty moves on my future wife, which ended up complicated and remotely hidden from my search for many years.

The tears puddled in her eyes as she tried to grab her purse. I stopped her with a light grasp. "I got this, babe."

"Then order two pieces of pecan pie to go and get me the hell out of here."

"Yes, Ma'am."

I pulled out my wallet and flipped my platinum card on the table as I made eyes at Tara. "That's a helluva card for a boy like yourself."

"I have a substantial bank account that my grandfather started."

She smiled and shook her head. "I don't even

want to know how much that beginning balance was."

"No," I replied, understanding that not all was fair or right in the world. I'd spent my childhood in a modest house but with what many would consider to be a silver spoon in my mouth.

Luxury came in the form of things—Mama's jewelry and fur coats and a new pair of Nikes on my feet every three months. We weren't jetting off to exotic locations, but we were quite spoiled. I never knew what it was like to struggle or live paycheck to paycheck. I never went to bed hungry for lack of food.

If I wanted something, I bought it. But when I chunked down a wad of cash for my first ride, I earned every dime slinging fish during the summers of high school.

"I got this."

A few minutes later, we hastily made our way to the exit, managing to avoid any social interactions, aside from the few brief waves of goodbye. Tara stopped us at the door. "Excuse me. I just saw the tip you left. Thank you so much."

"You're welcome," I said with a smile. I didn't fucking care. Money comes, and money goes, but brief moments of happiness and the memory they create—*that shit is priceless.*

We walked into the warm evening air when Trudy clutched my arm. "How much did you leave her?"

"Does it matter?"

"Ya," she said, stopping to grab a smoke. I lit it for her, and she handed me one. "Because girls like Tara don't usually make it out of their childhood nightmare. The path gets set in stone early on. Her mother was fourteen when she had Tara. And she has two already at twenty-one."

"A grand."

She rapidly blinked. "You gave her...*a thousand dollars?*"

"Ya." I flicked my brows. "I love spending blood money on the right people."

"I hate to say how happy that makes me," she said as we strolled towards the car. "Considering what I am spending on you."

"… Blood money?"

"Javi gives me a nice allowance from his *dealings*."

"That's blood money, sweetheart."

"Give me the keys," she demanded. I handed them over and opened her door. "I bought the house and my dogs with that money, too."

"And apparently, a boy toy for the weekend."

"A girl does what she has to do to get the job done."

I grinned. "I'll make sure you get your money's worth."

"You already have."

3

THE RIVER

There are undeniable similarities to Trudy and my lover boy. They have the same slight build and sharp jawline. Her eyes are almost ghost-like gray to his sad blues, but they're identical in shape and the way they use them to seduce and lure.

It should also be noted—they both drive like bats out of hell.

I'm all for flying on backroads, but Trudy put new meaning to holding on for your life.

She was wild and reckless, totally untamed. In essence, the perfect counterpart to my meticulously maddening OCD, her zestful energy poured fuel onto my embers, much like the gusts of Deacon's storms would spread my flames far and wide.

. . .

I noted the for sale sign in the yard as we pulled up to the house. "Are you moving?"

"I'm hoping to find a place closer to Juliet."

"Are you heavily involved in the scene?"

"No," she said, pulling into the garage as the dogs started cutting up in the backyard. "But I like the bar and the entertainment of the crowd. There is always something going on. The community is fun."

I didn't know much, but it sounded an awful lot like Ma Diaz had never worn a collar or held a whip —I couldn't rule either side out, so I asked, "Which are you?"

"I didn't bring you here for any other reason than to get on my knees in front of a hunk of a man, Darlin."

Oh. Fuck.

Sitting in the car, I was floored, ill-prepared, and stumped. I didn't know the first practical application of D/s, so I decided to wing it. "… Safeword?"

She stared over the steering wheel, considering my question, and whispered, "How about *Ride*?"

Now, at that point, I had zero clue her safeword was her son's moniker or the implication of such. I was innocent, and I must say, I do not advocate this practice. But for Trudy

—'all things in the interest of Deacon Cruz'—Diaz, it made sense. And what a way to stop a scene than by shouting your son's name…

I never claimed this story wasn't going to be fucked up; I only promised transparency.

You have earned that.

"Any limits?"

"If I got them, I don't know them," she muttered with a smile.

"Then let's find them—*together*."

"If I got them, I don't know them," would spin on repeat through my head because at no other point in my Dominant existence has someone ever said something so bluntly honest before entering a scene.

And the words were a glorious beginning for me. I immediately understood why Anna sent Trudy to me for counseling sessions.

Despite her experience in life, she was a newb. I was young. I could cut my teeth on Trudy Diaz in multiple ways. Her all-in-one package was almost like a lottery win. She handed over life lessons, and I blistered her ass.

With my respect for Anna growing monumentally by the

day, I accepted one thing—she was a woman to be feared. She could play matchmaker to detour the trajectory to line up her wins. She avoided losses by steering the pieces.

And therein, another lesson.

I learned as much about Anna Ford as I did by her selection of clients.

And I was a sponge, learning and growing, heading for the big show.

I just didn't know it at the time.

"Shall we go inside?"

"When was the last time you…"

"… Had sex?" With a wide grin, she laughed. "It's been a long fucking time."

My fingers brushed over hers, sitting on the gear shift. I leaned closer and softly kissed her lips. "Have you been waiting for me?"

"Like you can't imagine," she whispered against my lips as the heat rose. "I knew you would be here eventually."

I wish someone would've informed me.

My hand grazed over the top of her breast and slipped under the edge of the fabric as her eyes shuttered closed, and I kissed her again. My tongue flicked against hers, testing her invitation, and she swooped hers against mine. She was serious and not fucking around. I broke away. "Let's go."

Believing I could do this, I rubbed my sweaty palms on my jeans, and she shut the garage and unlocked the door. The second we stepped inside, she said, "Gabriel and Raphael, I'm home!"

I heard them at the back door as I pinned their ma against the wall with my mouth consuming hers. I stripped off her jacket and found salvation in her tender flesh. Lifting her arms high on the wall, she braced for impact.

I was eighteen.

I was starving.

And I was hard as a fucking stone.

My mouth devoured her neck as I spun her from the wall and sat her on the washing machine. "Oh shit, please don't turn it on."

"It's too late not to be turned on." I smirked, stripping off my shirt. Picking her leg up and bracing her foot on my thigh, I undid the many buckles on her boots. I loved unwrapping packages, and without a doubt, Trudy was one of the best wrapped ever. If I hadn't been so overly eager, I would have undone all those fasteners with my teeth because damn…I mean, *damn*.

I tossed the boots onto the jacket and unsnapped

her tauntingly evil silver chain belt as she lifted her hips, and I pulled the sparkling denim from her skin. "I bought nice lingerie for this event. Black panties with gold thread and a matching bra."

"You can wear them the rest of the weekend," I offered, peeling the lace from her hips, pulling her to the edge of the machine, and spreading her thighs. I dove in, head first, and my tongue skimmed over her slit, the perfect sweet dessert to finish off dinner.

I wouldn't start every encounter with a Raniero-tongue-lashing below the waist, but there was something about Trudy that demanded my attention focused on her pussy. Don't mistake me—I love a good pie, but it isn't high on my list with every woman. She must be special —extraordinary—to warrant tongue service.

The thing about it is once I go there, I cannot stop. So, it isn't a decision to take lightly. I must be willing to make the commitment and assess if my hound can make her come. Otherwise, it isn't worth it, but a woman releasing on my face is like nothing else. And when I achieve that rare prize, I hold onto her because nothing builds intimacy quite like cunnilingus.

There is a balance between giving and receiving, not

unlike getting a blow job. But if I am honest, I can jiz in anyone's mouth; it isn't that complicated. The stroking rhythm can all be controlled by the grip of hair and buck of hips.

Pussy is like a mysterious maze of wonder and enticement. And being able to make one come—on my tongue, fingers, dick—without any interaction from the owner is the gold standard and the pinnacle of sex challenges.

Patience is key.
Timing is everything.

Her fingers twisted in my hair, and she tilted back as a moan escaped from her decadent lips. "Don't …fucking…stop…Jesus…fucking…Christ…"

I rejoiced and held back a grin. I weaved my tongue around her clit with light brushes and pushed in one finger and then two.

Once nestled deep inside, I didn't hold back. I pumped with everything I had while keeping the delicate balance on her nub. Hard and soft. Fast and slow. In and out. Up and down. Over and over.

Her talons curled against my scalp. "Shit! What are you doing to me?"

What you paid me to do…

And doing it better than you've ever had, Ma'am.

Ignoring my needs, I refused her wiggling away with a firm grip to her ass cheek. An ass that I couldn't wait to spank, but only after the appetizer of her pussy saturated my tongue and proved what it could do in capable hands. I was an arrogant son of a bitch regarding sex even back then. I was good, and I knew I was—for one simple reason, I listened.

Trudy was a lonely middle-aged woman with a grown son and a club. And she was also ignored and invalidated, a stepping stone, and not much more. I dug deep with every twist of my forearm and elevated her from being trampled upon to being esteemed and high on *my* pedestal.

She was worth it.

Every fucking minute.

I have no idea how long I stayed between her thighs, drooling and salivating over her goods, but I was in no rush until I felt her tighten and slick my fingers with an upsurge of desire. And then, I brought it on like gangbusters pillaging a long-ago forgotten shelter. I reminded her of who she once was and what she had denied for so long.

She was a woman.

... *Fuck being a mother.*

... *Fuck being a wife.*

… Fuck being an old lady.

More than Deacon's mom, Javier's wife, and Delirium's Queen Bitch, she was a woman. And her name was Trudy.

Revere the woman and rebel against the labels.

And all I did was remind her of that…because I'm a nice guy…with a good tongue and steady hands. I wanted her screaming my name at the end of her orgasm because she deserved it.

Fuck me, I didn't matter.

This was all about her…her needs…her wants…her desires…her dreams she put aside for everyone else for so long. I was the gatekeeper for the flood of her very naughty girl.

And when I realized that, mid-fucking Trudy Diaz on her washing machine with something other than my demanding beast, I knew what my purpose was in The Contract. I was the happiness quotient Anna had been searching for. I took the little photo left in the drawer after the years of dust collected on the picture, and the edges frayed from neglect, and I stuck that motherfucking princess in a golden frame and put her high up on the mantle. That is what my job was—resurrection.

I was like a priest.

A holy man of women.

And it only worked because I gave a shit. Otherwise, I would've been every word they misspoke about me. I wasn't a slut down on Canal searching for the next big payout. I was needed. I was the one leading the lambs to the slaughter, and the massacre wasn't worth saving. I fired them up, one by one, and brought new meaning to the words: she's in her prime. We jointly smashed the shells life had made them and rebirthed them into sacred butterflies.

But it was more than just sex.

Way more.

"Fuck!" she screamed as I rubbed her spot just right and suckled upon her clit like a starved fledgling Dom.

Because I was.

Service went both ways, and I needed her trust if I was going to ask her to give up what I genuinely wanted—my hand on her ass and my grip on her throat.

But those rules—*they stay unspoken far too often.*

I came equipped knowing that balance was absolute because I had been smacked around and belittled and poked fun at my entire childhood. I understood it went both ways. Dom didn't mean tyrannical; sub didn't mean weak.

And Anna, God bless her soul, fostered that inherent belief in my soul where equality existed in all facets. Her coaching conversations enlivened me, spit-shined to be present, and ready to be put into practice. I was at the point of needing interactions to know if I would sink or swim. We required real-time data, and the only way to achieve that was in between Trudy Diaz's thighs.

Much later, I asked Trudy if she knew what she was getting into. With a smile, she merely replied, "What are you talking about, sugar? I volunteered."

I was a handful—a hot mess of a boy looking to be a man—and I knew it. What I didn't realize is how much I needed these women to shape me. My reference points for women growing up were as conflicted as they come.

On one side, I had my protesting, feminist, outspoken Nonna.

And on the other, the diminishment of femininity by my father, which my mama and sisters pandered.

Both ways.

Everything goes both ways.

My mama accepted my father's violence, setting an

example for my sisters' future tormented relationships, while I fought against his establishment. And it was precisely that. Everyone feared Cesario Raniero, including me. But I vowed never to be that man.

As fucked up as my primary female role model was, the male was equally bad.

And Anna made provisions for that.

But I digress… We're getting there soon enough.

Her hands dropped to my shoulders as she held me in place. She didn't need to. I had managed to get her this far, and I wasn't giving up yet.

In the dark house, we made silent pacts to one another, promises kept with complete discretion, and made vows to continue our tryst. We were falling for one another fast, not in a romantic sense, but in a way where love bloomed without bounds. We spilled over the edges and tore down the walls. It didn't matter if she was an old lady or that I was a mafioso's son. None of it counted. The only thing that mattered between her and me was that we were both humans.

We built on that.

Fuck the labels. Break the rules. Cross the borders. And scribble outside of the lines.

But I knew as I was tongue deep in between her lush lips that she would defend my ass—*and likely pull a blade*—if it came to that. And without a doubt, I would defend her interests against my father.

In many ways, she was my first negotiation, merger, and acquisition. And everyone who came after Trudy had a whole lot of catching up to do. It was pure brilliance by Anna to align with the bitch that ran the books for Delirium because she got me in with her baby trades.

Crate of guns for double?

Sure, here's my account. Take what you need.

It was all gambling, risk assessment, and strategy. I funded her efforts, and we reaped magnificent rewards of Javier Diaz and Saint Cruz. Together—Trudy and me—we are unstoppable.

She is the epitome of a hustler, unlike her son.

Deacon can shuffle, but he doesn't do it often because he's surrounded by those who do it with sheer ease. I've watched Trudy toss down cases of my money on the desk of guys who would just as soon she was six feet under, all to swing a deal and create a network. She was Sal Raniero's head cheerleader long before I knew I needed a whole squad.

And the squad became a team, and the team turned into the devout.

The troop was ever-expanding, and I generously provided for her—few people knew who had his fingers deep in her pussy and lined her bank account. The ice on her skin, I did that too.

It is important to note—she was the only "client" who earned such privileges.

And that goes back to Anna, believing and trusting in Trudy.

So, our start that night in her laundry room blossomed into so much more than mere sex. You need to understand my loyalty to Trudy and her son are far different and separate entities. And it is also worth mentioning that I appreciate my position in her life.

…all things in the interest of Deacon Cruz…

I am…was…and will always be…expendable for one in her eyes, so it's Deacon first, me second, and the rest of the world against Trudy. I'll take the odds.

"Salvatore…" she whispered, digging those nails into my shoulders. "I'm going to…" She eagerly bucked against my ample thrusts and relentless tongue as she soared into blissful ecstasy. Her orgasm erupted like a beautiful fountain of fireworks, and I slurped every drop from her cavern. In the desert of my father's lands for so long, I was dying of thirst, and she quenched every trace of self-doubt with one deliriously right moment. "Shit… What the hell did we just do?"

My scruff was soaked with her juices when I peered up. "We signed the deal."

Her smile ticked up at one corner—the same crooked grin I would fall for on her son—and she locked her fingers with mine. "We did." I was throbbing in my jeans, but it didn't matter. I trusted my time would come. "I'm going to go clean up a little, and I'll meet you in the living room."

I helped her down from the washer and handed her clothes and boots over. "Thank you, Trudy."

"For?" She nervously skirted away with a light blush on her cheeks. "What did I do?"

"You trusted me."

"Always, Sally boy." She winked, and I smiled.

"I'm going to go have a smoke."

"Oh, feel free to smoke in here, just crack a window or the door. You can let the dogs in," she said, nodding with an uncertainty. I could tell I knocked her off her game by the brief interlude and broke through her toughened exterior. It was clear by her skittishness; not many people managed to penetrate her emotional fortress. "And help yourself to a beer in the fridge or anything from the bar."

Running my hand through my hair, I lowered my head, licked my lips, and glanced up at her walking off before I ventured into the great room—kitchen, nook, and living room all in one. Clicking on all the lights, she disappeared into her bedroom upstairs.

I splashed some water on my face and hair in her kitchen sink. Taking a deep breath, I rubbed my eyes before drying up and ruffling my curls. I pulled a smoke from the back pocket of my jeans and opened the back door to let her beautiful fur babies inside. They sniffed my hand and chased after Trudy as I caught sight of the rows of pictures lining every available space in the living area. I flicked my Zippo and studied each one as I paced closer.

Deacon Cruz was hands down the most gorgeous male ever conceived—*this was my first thought*. From his baby pictures with bright platinum hair through fumbling teenage years in grunge wear to more recent images on a motorcycle, out on a boat fishing, and grinning like he had a whole closet full of skeletons. I picked a picture up that wasn't in a frame. And then it hit me—*hard*.

Deacon was only two years and a few months older than me.

Two years, four months, and four days if we're exact.
And I just skyrocketed his mother into nirvana.
Oh. Fuck.
I was an asshole.
And he was going to fucking kill me.

"You want to see his baby book?" she asked, startling me. "He was the only child I managed to raise."

"How many do you have?"

"That's a story for the bottom of a whiskey bottle, but let's just say—*I have three.*" In her pink silk nightgown, she slowly approached. "That was right before he was sent to the slammer. That was his girlfriend at the time…" I stared at the picture of beauty. Her long hair and eyes were captivating against his ruggedly masculine qualities. "Maybe I should say, fuck buddy…my boy ran up a hell of a tab with that whore. His father almost put a hit on his head."

The girl was a whore.

Or so I believed because Trudy said so.

As it turned out, Trudy believed every human of the female persuasion that she didn't deem suitable for the one precious son she did raise was a whore or some other derogatory term. She liked no one Deacon brought home. Well, only one…and Trudy happened to like fucking him. Don't worry, she didn't discriminate and called me a manwhore plenty of times.

And I was a foolish, foolish young man.

The girl in the picture was a trained operative, who preferred being called a tension relief specialist, and the granddaughter of one of the most substantial international outfits.

Oh, and she ended up being the girl of my dreams.

But alas, that isn't why we're here.

We're here because Trudy Diaz was ten-seconds from pulling out Deacon's baby book, and I was strangely fascinated by her and him. The comparisons between he and I— the club kid and the mafia son—both with the heavy burdens of expectations.

He ran off at sixteen; I ran off at eighteen.

We were running side by side, away from our father's stronghold, and yet, we had never met. We never crossed paths. I had briefly met his father, Victor "Saint" Cruz, once in New York, as I tagged along—more like my father tugged me by my ear—to a clandestine midnight meeting.

At thirteen, I didn't pay much attention to the business details, but on the drive home, I knew things didn't go well. My father was fuming with rage when he pulled off to the shoulder. We were on an empty backroad with no one around for miles. He marched out onto the bridge before us, slowly turning to face the river, the fog, and me.

The kiss of a harsh north wind burned my cheeks as I waited by the car. I crept closer, entranced by the stunning visual of my robust father gazing into the darkness. One good heave-ho and I could topple the menace of society into the chilled rushed river. I didn't think about what the explanation needed to be. All I thought was how easy it would be.

On my approach, he warned, "You must never trust him."

"Because he's from the South?"

"No, because he's a snake."

Pot calling the kettle black?

"I'll keep that in mind."

"It's more than keeping it in mind!" my father yelled, yanking me by the overcoat and pushing my back to bend over the guardrail. I didn't fight. Feeling the wind blow through my curls, I tilted my head and stared at the water. There were rocks and branches and debris. Logic said I wouldn't make it, but I knew I could. "You've got to play the cards we've been dealt and be prepared to pull out the ones we've kept hidden for years! This isn't just a joke anymore!"

I already understood.

I understood because I had been with him when he stomped into Tommy Giordano's house and killed his wife and three young children in cold blood—as a warning.

I understood because where ordinary people had dishes of pillow mints, we had containers of bullets and walls of pictures that were replaced by stacks of cash hidden behind fake art in expensive frames.

I understood because everyone connected to my father feared him, and when things didn't go as he expected, his violence spread like wildfire.

He managed to take my grandfather's establishment and turn it into a cheap and seedy back alley gang. He wasn't just a mobster, but a bully, extorting money and raising mayhem on every block. His hunger for power overshadowed every moral fiber in his being.

And this was what I was expected to do.

This is what I was raised for.

"I will remember," I mumbled, praying he tossed me over the edge so I would have a chance to getaway…to escape…to break free from his enslavement." I will remember."

"Stay away from Saint and his devil spawn!"

Takes one to know one.

And I wouldn't forget.

Replacing the photo, I innocently blinked at Trudy. "Tell me all about your son."

At that exact moment, I became more than the teenage runaway. I was a traitor. I was a defector. I was leaving and abandoning my post. It would take years to figure out how to dismantle his machine, but I mentally checked out that day in Trudy Diaz's house, surrounded by pictures of her son.

And there was not a goddamned thing my father could do about it.

4

THE PULSE OF FEAST OR FAMINE

IN HER CLAWFOOT TUB, TRUDY AND I TALKED for hours over a bottle of wine, two joints, and a pack of smokes. Two dozen candles lit the room up like a sanctuary.

And confess, she did.

She was an open book just looking for someone to listen while I said very little except for the occasional question for clarification.

And hustling with sweet talk worked like a charm on the lonely.

That night I could've put an end to Delirium, Reckless Rebellion, and Saint Cruz's operation if I was a spiteful player. I could've gone back to Daddy, told him everything I knew, and he would've had his goons infiltrating their jurisdiction in less than three months.

But I had a bigger fish to fry.

My own blood.

"Why does Deacon not want Delirium?"

Trudy laughed. "No one wants Delirium. It's a mess. And there is no way Javi would ever give it to Deacon. He's the byproduct of my affair with a man he can't stand." She shook her head and inhaled on the cigarette. "But he has no problem in taking Saint's dope and bangs and profiteering off of him."

"There is no loyalty," I mused, running my damp fingers through my wet curls and polishing off the last of the wine in my glass. "It is *everything*."

"You should know something, Sal," she said, licking her lips. "It's not always black and white."

I understood the point but not where she was coming from. "What do you mean?"

"My son is exactly like his father."

I shifted my glance to her panicked expression. "He…he's friendly, babe."

"I think I'm a nice guy too.

"No…not like this…I'm pretty sure he's gay or at least questioning his…you know, sexuality."

I wasn't sure what to say, so I opted for the one thing I did know. "He'll be safe with me."

"Do you promise?" With mascara staining beneath her eyes, she begged. "I don't care if you want to beat the crap out of him for the shit he does in the game, but don't punish him for this."

"… Did Javi?"

"After beating the crap out of him for being with some football jock, Javi sent his ass to a skanky club whore that next weekend. His version of conversion therapy and brainwashing was in stale old cooch. It's no wonder he's sitting on the fence."

Sitting on the fence gives quite the view.

"Did you ask Deacon what happened?" She rubbed her lips together and gazed at the bubbles. "Trudy, I need to know what I'm getting into…"

"He was on his knees and about to give the guy head. It was the teams' way of hush money. They found Deacon with some other kid that he liked and, in an effort, to keep the team quiet, Deacon offered…services. I'm pretty sure he was turning tricks in Chicago."

While Ma was reliving the shock, I was thinking…

Deacon Cruz. Skilled. Negotiator.

"He got them weed and booze and entertained the captain," she said, using the tip of her cigarette to light another. "He took off shortly after all of that went down, and I only found out after the fact. You know better than anyone how well that shit flies in our world, and I need to know you aren't going to use it against him."

I may use it, but not against him.

"I don't give a shit who he is getting his rocks off with as long as he can move stock."

"He can…he will…just give me a bit to work on him."

"Does he blame you?"

Tears filled her eyes. "I blame myself more than he does, but he kept me out of it. If I would've known Javi beat him up for that crap, he wouldn't still be breathing."

"Shame."

"Tell me," she said with a smirk. Tears trickled over her cheeks as she shook her head. "I did everything I could do to shield that boy. And when shit went down, I was always conveniently sent somewhere else. Javi knew how to play me until Deacon left, and he lost his leverage."

We stayed quiet for a long bit, thinking and staring at one another. "Are all three children Saint's?"

"I don't know. The twins…" Her eyes rapidly closed as she stumbled and said too much. "Well, no sense in keeping that a secret now. The twins

—*Diablo and Deacon*—belong to Saint. My daughter is either Saint's or Javi's, but I haven't seen her since I gave birth in Mexico."

I furrowed my brow. "You went South of the border?"

"Ya," she reluctantly confided. "I was six months pregnant and barely showing. Things had been escalating in my relationship with Javi, so I sent Deacon away for summer camp."

Stop. Rewind that—

Deacon's "summer camp" was three months in Arizona in a Cinco safehouse, smoking weed, playing video games, and watching porn. He was eleven—and Cinco had some standards, including Sunday mass and no fornication or killing before the age of fifteen.

I know their handbook well.

But I also know Deacon.

And he learned the fine art of stealing cars and swiping clothes from the mall. He loved to shop even when he had no money.

"I went away for three months, had a cesarean in some dank shack, and came back home."

"Jesus Christ…and Deacon doesn't know?"

"He thinks his only half-sibling is Wendy, and I went away to have some illicit peacekeeping affair with a cartel leader at Javi's request," she said, puffing like a chimney. "Deacon doesn't know about either sibling."

"What did you tell Javi?"

"That I needed to get away for a while before I killed him seemed to be enough of a reason."

"Holy Mother of God, this is a mess…" I leaned my head back and glared at the tin ceiling. "What do you want me to do?"

"Find her if you can."

My head sprung forward. "Find her? You want me to find your daughter?"

"Ya, I mean, not today or tomorrow, but that is the only thing I want from you."

Despite knowing how much I need Trudy on my team, I grimaced at the thought of hunting down a kid. "When was she born?"

"August 5, 1999."

"You had her early."

"I had her at barely eight months," she said, making no excuses for her bad choices. "I never even held her."

"Shit. So, you want me to locate your almost

nine-year-old daughter in exchange for…"

"Anything you want," she pleaded, inching across the tub. Her fingers eased around my dick, and I quickly responded to her touch. I pulled her up to straddle over me, and I thrust deep inside of her hot cunt as water splashed onto the floor. "Just keep my kids safe. Protect them at all costs."

Trudy Diaz was damn lucky to have been first because I humored her more than anyone else. And if truth be told, she was probably the reason I ended up getting involved with Deacon. "Protect them at all costs."

We were never just client and escort, but partners, conspiring to keep her children standing in a war zone. She knew I had a warrior in me even when I wasn't so sure.

"What about Diablo?" I growled, needing to come. "You want him safe too?"

"There is no saving him." She tilted back in my arms. "He's a lost cause. Saint already tried to straighten him out after his second arrest."

"So, you have the vindictive sinner, the future saint, and the missing daughter?"

"Yes," she snickered. "Help me. And I will help you more than you think an old bag ever could."

"You're not an old bag," I assured, gripping her ass and bouncing her on my cock. "But you play a mean ass game, Ms. Diaz."

"You only want bad bitches on your team, Salvatore."

"Do they all come with such a mess?"

"Yes," she whispered, biting her lip. "And they'll be fucking loyal to you like no other *most* of the time. I've been amid this scene most of my life, and it isn't the guys detonating like a land mine. I've seen more old ladys and scorned bitches pulling a blade or popping a gun than any man. It gets *personal* with women. Real fucking quick. Especially if their children are involved."

"Mama Bear and her cubs?"

"Grizzly-fucking-bear and her hellions." Her fingers moved from the edge of the tub to my shoulders. "Fuck me, Raniero. And let me guide your way through the maze."

"I'm going to come soon."

"Do it, Sally."

She was the light in the darkness.

Much like her son.

Everything I have today goes back to Trudy Diaz, offering to carry my ass into the fray. And still, I accept the second fiddle because I owe her…and I will always owe her.

I've tried to imagine where I would be without her, but I can't. Anna couldn't very well have coached me on interpersonal communications in the mafia because she was heavily involved forty years ago, and it was a different world now. She chose the best bitch of the current bunch to be my number one.

THE NEXT MORNING, I WOKE UP TO THE smell of bacon and steak. My belly rumbled as I stumbled out of bed, took a piss, and noticed a pile of clean clothes and a note on the bathroom counter.

"They're Deacon's. They should fit. Yours are in the wash. Take a shower. And come to see me, Sir."

I fumbled through the stack of ripped jeans, a black t-shirt, socks, and boxers. "Shit…"

My fingers brushed over the denim and picked at one of the loose strands, and then I did something I'll never forget. I took a hot fucking shower and wore another man's underwear for the first and last time.

. . .

... Was it early crushing?

Probably but not in the way you're likely thinking. I had zero interest in men at that point. Deacon was beautiful, but I was secure enough in myself, and that was an okay thing to admit without there being strings attached to it. I'd signed the contract with Jack Kerris and thought he was quite handsome too.

But not to the point where I wanted to consent to bend over.

We're getting to the point of my sexual awakening…no worries.

Deacon got out without any strings. He had freedom, and he had it made. Or so I believed at the time. He held the Holy Grail.

Honestly, I was more jealous than anything, and being a superstitious bastard, I decided that wearing his clothes couldn't hurt, and maybe some of his free-flying would rub off on me.

Well, something was about to get rubbed off, but it damn sure wasn't Deacon's goodness and light. It was the thing I least expected and what I most needed—even more than Trudy Diaz.

I just didn't know it yet.

. . .

"Well, the clothes seem to fit," she said in the kitchen as I surfaced from the bedroom. She poured me a cup of coffee. "Did you sleep well?"

"Ya, great."

"Sit down," she suggested, waving her hand to the nook. "How do you take your coffee?"

Taking a seat, I acknowledged everything I did yesterday played into today. It was a strange concept for eighteen, knowing outcomes were affected by actions, but everything I put into her yesterday had the potential to grow today.

Plant the seeds before your ass is hungry.

"In a mug?" I snorted. "Anyway, it is fine unless it's sweetened."

She grinned and giggled. "I gotcha, Darlin."

Sitting the cup down on the table, I noted the enormous ruby and diamond ring on her finger, and I grabbed her hand. "It's not from Javi."

"You have a lover?"

"I have a long-distance admirer," she said, blushing and walking back to the kitchen. "But I'm not playing his game."

"Is it serious?"

"What?" She shook her head. "He'll send flowers, chocolates, booze, fur coats, and jewelry about once every three months, and I send an appropriate thank you note."

"Have you dated this fellow?"

"You don't date Delarte Cristos, honey." Immediately, I recognized the name—Nicky's father. His business as a shipping magnate slid into the underworld more than once, and by the size of that rock, his eyes were on one prize, Trudy Diaz. After placing a plate of food in front of me, she sat down and lifted her brows with a glowing smile. "He wants me to do for him what I am doing for you."

"Thank you, Ma'am."

"You're welcome, sugar." She took a sip of coffee and propped her elbows on the table. "Look, I don't need an old jalopy. I need a hot, new machine. And Ma can't be bought by pretty things. His gifts mean nothing because his focus isn't me."

Cristos would never put Deacon or anyone else above Nico. *Ever.*

And Trudy knew it.

If Trudy served as my criminal affairs finishing school, then she owned me—lock, stock, and barrel. She knew it, and now, I knew it. And apparently, Anna knew it too.

Catch the Boston Kid before someone else does because he will make trouble one day.

"What is his focus?"

She pulled a cigarette from her pack. I swiftly grabbed the lighter and flicked the flame. "Thanks," she exhaled. "My best guess is he wants Deacon's swing vote."

"… Swing vote?"

"You're both—my son and you—loose cannons… swing votes. A young package with a lot of potential. No one honestly believed you would stay by Raniero's side. And no one ever thought Deacon would run to his Dad's wing. Getting either of you is a win for someone."

I picked up a piece of bacon draped over the steak. "… And if you get both of us?"

"Then, I hit the fucking jackpot."

Ironically, on my first-weekend escort, we didn't spend the whole day fucking but connecting on a profound spiritual level while shopping.

It was far more important than money shots.

After I cleaned up breakfast and fed Gabriel and Raphael the leftover steak, I followed her out to the garage, where she opened the door and uncovered a sweet vintage bike. "Can you ride?"

"Are you safewording or asking a legit question?" I smirked, and she thumped my shoulder. "I can."

"If you ever need a bike, the code for the garage is 1225."

Deacon's birthday.

"Thank you," I said, meandering out into the driveway. "Is the house really for sale?"

"Only for the right price," she admitted, stealing a drag of the cigarette from my fingers. "It's more of a cover to make Javi believe I am working on the family unit."

"The family meaning the club."

"You got it," she said. "The only family I have on my mind rests in the hands of two precious souls, and I'm looking at one."

I scanned over her property and out to the road. It was remote. "You think I can save you."

"Wrong," she corrected, swiping the smoke from my hand. Her eyes met mine. "I know you can. How about we go out?"

"Where to?"

"Austin, Dallas, hell a casino in Shreveport…"

I grinned. "Anywhere but here?"

"Anywhere but here."

I gave her a side-eyed glance and grinned. "Am I driving?"

"Yes, Sir."

Half an hour later, I'm behind the wheel of her swanky truck in my sunglasses and flying down the freeway with her in the passenger seat. I had no idea where we were going. We headed west through dusty towns and swaths of dying farmlands.

She held my hand tight as we sang every hair-band song. I didn't think about anything involving my father. I just acted, running on pure emotion. My thoughts turned to Charlotte and her new boyfriend. I'd kill him if he hurt her. And then, I thought of Trudy's dogs and how they seemed to like me. I feared the son's bite more than the pits.

And that wasn't totally off base, either.

We finally stopped in some little town that had their main thoroughfare blocked off for *Garage Sale Days*.

We ate deliciously greasy burgers from a dive. She shopped, nudging for the better deals, and I carried all her bags. It was mostly junk, but a lot can be said by the junk a person keeps. She was happy, and I wasn't half bad. I was screwing a woman more than two and a half times my age, but she didn't act fifty. Hell, she didn't even act thirty. She was flirty and frivolous with the sellers. We were having a good time until…

"Trudy…"

She quickly turned to five guys in unmarked cuts. "Emiliano!"

Now, this is important because I've never told another soul what I am about to tell you. And you need to know because if something ever randomly happens to me, it may all lead back to this "fluke" encounter with one badass motherfucker.

She hugged the gruff looking man tight. He was wearing a cut and looked like he'd seen some shit. "This is Sal."

"Of the…" he said with a heavy accent.

"Of *the*," Trudy replied with a wink as I extended my hand like a polite young man.

"Emiliano Navarro. Ecuador."

The three words of his introduction had my knees shaking. He didn't need to say more. He was cartel, and Trudy gushed like he hung the damn moon.

I felt trapped as he firmly gripped my hand. "Salvatore Raniero. Italiano."

"Boston." He smiled. "You'll come to church tonight."

I wasn't sure what he was referring to, but I followed Trudy's lead as she asked, "What time?"

"Angela and the ladies are cooking," he said. "How about seven?"

"We'll be there."

He put his sunglasses on and disappeared into the crowd. "Who was that?"

"Emiliano Navarro," she repeated his name, giving no information. She leaned in closer. "He's a hitman for the cartel."

"Which one?"

She shrugged. "Whoever is paying the highest?"

"Fuck."

"You need him," she informed with a profound resolve. I picked up my pace and marched towards her truck, parked with hundreds of others in an abandoned grocery store lot. "Where are you going?"

"Home!"

"Oh, no!" she said as I put my back against the truck. "You aren't going home. You need him. You may not think you do, but you do. You need all of them. From the top of the cake to the crumbs on the floor, you need it all."

Yes, she compared criminal hierarchy to cake.

"Why do I need to break bread with a fucking Ecuadorian assassin?"

"Because you never know when you might need him."

"I'm not issuing a hit on anyone," I muttered, setting her bags in the cab of the truck and lighting a smoke. "At least, not that I know of…"

"It doesn't matter, Raniero. Someone could issue one on your ass, and if he knows you, he'll stop it."

I dug through the bags to find my new ball cap because I didn't think to bring mine. I didn't know I'd be doing anything more than getting my rocks off. I yanked the tags and put it on backward while my jaw furiously popped. I was beyond angry. "I don't want this…"

"It doesn't matter what you want," she replied, cornering me. "You don't seem to understand any more than Deacon does, you do not have a choice in the matter. You can play the game or be terminated. There are no other options."

"There has to be."

"You want to stroll up to the Feds and see if they'll give you protection? I'll tell you how well that worked when we bury you. Pull your head out of your ass and stop thinking that you must be him. Nowhere is it written that you have to model yourself after Cesario, but you need to be doing something, or you're just a sitting duck."

I hated it—all of it. "For no other reason than I'm his son?"

"For no other reason than you are his son."

"… Dinner?"

"You'll love it—empanadas and ceviche." She grinned with that maternal smile. The same one that said eat your vegetables because they're good for you and after two years of metal wearing into your cheeks that your teeth will be beautiful. It was a fucking nightmare, and I was living it.

Feeling irritated by the whirlwind situation, I glanced around the parking lot. It was full of empty cars as people shopped the afternoon away. And I found a crutch in controlling the only thing I could. My fetish came to light and made the poison go down easier. "Get in the truck and suck my fucking dick until I come."

"I'd love to, Sir."

5

PEOPLE NEED PEOPLE

"Sweet boy," Trudy whispered, touching my cheek as I napped in the passenger seat. She drove to the church after swallowing every last drop of my rage. I was still a bit pissed, but I was at least willing to work the situation. "We're here."

Let me add, Bitch gave a helluva a persuasive blowjob.

I peered out the window at the incredible white cathedral surrounded by a dark purple sky. "Holy fuck, it's a church."

"I wasn't taking you to a club meeting." She opened the water and handed it to me. "You're going to be fine. You need these people. They put on their pants just like you."

"I have precum stains on your son's underwear," I randomly announced without warning.

"Ya?"

"… Don't you think this is all a little weird?"

"Oh, Darlin, you ain't seen nothing yet." She squeezed my hand, hopped out with a pep in her step, and walked around to open my door. She had to get the baby—me—out of the car seat because I was as stubborn as a mule. "Come on. Don't be shy."

"He's an assassin."

"Stop worrying about his kill count," she pointed out. "He isn't aiming at you, nor is he going to be if you will get your ass out of the truck, and come inside."

Turning in the seat, I propped my feet on the threshold, maintaining my ground, and lighting a smoke. "Cruz won't listen to you." On my insinuation, she crossed her arms. "Tell me the truth."

"Deacon wants nothing to do with any of it. That is why I suggested sending him off to New Orleans to get schooled by an expert."

I sighed with frustration. "… While his mother is giving me private lessons?"

"I am trying to save two rambunctious boys from making very critical—*grave*—mistakes which could adversely affect the rest of their lives."

"I have no power," I mumbled, growing more agitated by the minute. "There has been an outage."

"Bullshit, Sal." Her arms uncurled as she jetted out her hip and smacked her hand on it. *Oh. Shit. Pissed off Mama stance.* "You're both blind as fucking bats. Neither one of you seems to want to rise to the challenge."

"I'll rise to the fucking challenge, but not this one."

"Hello! Hello!" Emiliano shouted from across the way. "Welcome to the church!"

Trudy waved and smiled as he strolled over. "He's a little wet behind the ears."

"I am not!" I argued on the verge of a tantrum.

Emiliano stepped between Trudy and me and lightly grasped my shoulders. "Hey, it's just a meal. Come eat. Don't offend Angela. She's been cooking all day."

"I mean no disrespect to your wife."

"She isn't my wife, daego," he interjected. "She is my sister. Make no assumptions."

"I apologize, Sir." He braced his hand on my forearm and assisted me out of the vehicle. It was oddly compassionate as I stepped down, and he embraced me tightly. "Are you really an assassin?"

"I am really your new familia."

. . .

The Church is an incredible piece of architecture in Godland. The wooden vessel at one time housed Baptists and then Methodists until both outgrew the space and built in Sugargrove. It is near La Chiesa, the mission, where I have had numerous dealings until its recent demise.

Thousands of towns popped up at the turn of the last century, filled to the brim with hopes and dreams. Not all these hamlets survived, but the remnants of the past do.

When I first met Emiliano Navarro, the fairgrounds were still in operation on the weekends. Attendance was dwindling, but it was good old-fashioned fun. Cotton candy and Caramel corn filled the air as kids ran wild.

You're probably wondering where this is going, but trust me—this entry is worth it.

Back in the nineties, Godland took a hard hit when two rivaling gangs battled it out between the merry-go-round and the house of mirrors. Four innocent people were killed, and the population plummeted from almost six thousand to five hundred.

Javier Diaz, Trudy's husband, started the war as he wanted to expand and encroach into Anna's town.

Who stopped it?

One man who just so happened to be good friends with Emiliano Navarro.

That's who.

Godland exists as a ghost town now, except for the

shadowy strangers showing up once a blue moon. They drew lines, served up retribution, and made bodies vanish. And Navarro and his gang were very good at what they did.

And as much as I didn't want to admit it, Trudy was right. I needed Navarro in my toolbox. There were a million ways to handle the vermin.

Nico had his niche carved out—no pun intended—but it wasn't my preference. Navarro was clean, quiet, calculating like a bird of prey, swooping from the sky and attacking with a vicious assault. There would be a whole lot of blood spilled before anyone knew.

In and out.

They were good and killed like others fucked—to get the job done. The most impressive part of Navarro and his troop is how fluidly they danced without words. They knew one another's tics, habits, and issues, and they buffed those to an indecipherable blur. They knew how to smudge and compensate for each other. If nothing else, Navarro was an ideal template for which to base my goals for The Unholy upon.

Trudy was right.

In a world of sloppy meals served up by street thugs, Navarro and his militia were a shining five-star seamlessly executed. We learn by example, and my father's lessons were flawed from the start.

A time will come when Navarro and I are no longer friends, but foes...rivals...enemies. To be the best, the student must outperform the teacher. The crowning achievement is to need the lessons no longer and want to challenge the man.

And that is a massive part of the reason we're doing this.

You may not read this until many years after the gun goes off, but if I'm not issuing the delivery and end up receiving, these words will be all you have left of me. I've been a vampire for far too long, sucking the life out of souls and discarding them with the refuse, and eventually, I'll sink into a lethal meal.

I pray it doesn't come in the form of Navarro.

I'm prepared to go down, but I want to be better than him.

And I want you to be better than him…because you are.

You are far better than I could ever be.

I'm a shit starter, and you're a minister.

Preach the gospel as only you can.

"Do you like the cold up North?" Navarro asked as he sat directly across the table from me over plates of flavorful meats and tangy sauces. "Because I cannot stand it."

I finished chewing, took a gulp of my water, and replied, "I don't particularly care for the climate."

"Neither do I," he hissed. "Especially when I don't get paid."

"Pardon?"

"Your father purchased some services from me and has refused to pay, daego."

My mouth opened, shocked by being cornered, but not surprised by my father's actions. "What do you want me to do?"

"I want you not to return to your father."

"I didn't plan on it," I respectfully replied.

"Because I don't want to have to kill you."

I shifted my gaze along the length of the table as everyone went silent. They were waiting on the response of a kid living in a dirty man's world, but there were tricks to the game—play the poker face, speak the lies and believe them, and never let the other pieces scattered on the board see your emotions.

I felt Trudy, sitting next to me, grab my thigh, but I didn't waver or flinch. She didn't need to get involved in this pissing contest. It was between Navarro and me. A test to see the worth of a man.

"Would you like me to do it for you?"

He hastily jetted back in his chair as my response threw him off. He scanned my expression and examined the seriousness of my thought. "… Kill yourself?" I pursed my lips together, lifted a brow, and cocked my head as my jaw fired up grinding rounds. "You're fucking insane," he stoically declared, deeming my words valid. His composure broke into a bout of hysterical laughter. "I like this boy! Get my best fucking tequila out!"

With his men celebrating, I snarled at Trudy as she whispered, "Shit. You fucking scared me."

"There is a fine line."

"Be careful with that one," she warned, predicting a future I couldn't see. "Keep it tethered taut because you're fucking dangerous."

Several hours later, in the pantry room, the sweltering heat poured from the kitchen into the minuscule space barely capable of holding the twin bed. Stocked shelves lined the walls with row after row of vegetables, fruits, and meats. The church was a safe house, a bunker, and a place far removed from Navarro's sandbox.

From the next room, the partying laughter echoed through the shiplap siding. The window was open wide, but the breeze was non-existent and seemed to add to the humidity. My back was sticky and wet as my hands dug into the supple flesh, and I searched for absolution while staring at cans of creamed corn.

The woman beneath me moaned, "Fuck me, Salvatore. Fuck me. Hard."

Angela Navarro only spoke three words of English—*fuck me* and *hard*.

Sweating buckets, I soaked the thin sheet covering the bed and signed a deal for my entire future based on the splooge in my dick.

A few years older than I, Angela whispered to her brother at dinner after my highly regarded play of words. By the time the plates were cleared, he had announced, "My sister would like to fuck you."

It was straightforward. Very blunt. Very bold.

O—kay.

I smiled with an uncertainty, still believing in the romantic notions of first dates over coffee. I should've thrown those out the window because those ideals went as flat as Trudy's teased up mess of hair in the furnace of a hot Texas summer.

People did not tell Emiliano Navarro, no.

What was I going to say?

I'm sorry I can't fuck your sister because I'm a male escort?

I glanced at Trudy, slightly crossfaded on booze and bud, and she swung her hand. "Go ahead. Git'r done." She winked as Angela smiled from the kitchen door. Trudy grabbed my arm. "Consider it prepayment for services rendered."

"Shouldn't she be paying me?"

"Not this time, sweetheart."

This was not in the contract.

Not even the fine print.

I wish I could tell you how atrocious she was, but Angela Navarro was fucking beautiful—long mocha hair and beguiling hazel eyes with a rack that demanded attention. And God, she could cook…and fuck.

She lived in a border town with the rest of Navarro's cronies and cared for her brother like no one else. At times, she would follow him into South America for his longer stays and prepare grandiose spreads for his team.

See, I didn't realize it at eighteen, but Navarro wasn't just one man with a silencer and good aim. At any point, he has a good twenty guys working for him that no one will ever see.

His infantry is a perplexing dynamic of infrastructure based on his keen ability to get the job done, but everything comes at a price.

Angela ended up disappearing in 2014.

Some would blame Navarro's work while others

contended something more sinister was in play—that he had sold or traded her to the Mexican cartel—Immortal—in exchange for his living to see another day.

I had different thoughts on the matter, having spent many meals with Navarro and his men. Keep in mind, our first meeting that night at the church was in 2008. Over those six years, before Angela went missing, I got to know the guy. He loved his sister, and there was no way he handed her over without a fight. He gave her to me that night—one night—because she asked.

I also considered another darker alternative—she wanted out and sold him down the river. She had an arsenal full of his intel, which would've been priceless for the right buyer, and there was only a select handful who could afford her knowledge—Immortal, Lotus, and The Commission.

Yes, I wrapped the package. Thank God.

You will find no Raniero-Navarro offspring running about, I assure you. And I know this with absolute certainty because I saw her several more times that year. She was warm and welcoming but treated me more like a brother than a lover. Odd? Very.

Fucking Angela was a rite of initiation into his army.

Bang his sister, and she likes you, you become familia.

Bang his sister, and she doesn't like you, you don't leave the compound.

… And I'd been privy to that happening more than once.

. . .

"Stop!" She pushed against my shoulders and smiled. I'd never had trouble coming before, but I'd never fucked in a 120°F room either. It might have been hotter. I didn't have the cognitive capacity to determine the temperature in hell's butthole.

But damn, it was hot.

I could've blamed the bizarre setting with the audience of green beans and beets, but it all boiled down to genetics. I'm naturally hot-natured, sweat at the first hint of warmth, and the system shuts down and goes into safe mode for self-preservation.

Luckily, Angela was an expert at dealing with men whose veins filled with radiating fire. She understood my south of the border brethren better than most.

She rose from the bed, wrung out a towel in the basin, and wiped me down. "Salvatore…*hot*."

Angela was up to five words and counting, but still, we weren't getting anywhere fast through verbal communication. I loved how she inflected my name in her Ecuadorian tongue and how slick her hollow melded against my shaft.

"Very," I said panting. "Hot."

With tenderness, she rinsed and repeated the process until I calmed—the heat, the stress, the mess I was in. It all played into my performance with Angela. She trailed her finger down the center of my chest and stopped at my heart. "Love."

I thought she was asking if I was *in* love. "No one."

"Love," she muttered, blinking at my dick and grinning. I briefly thought she wanted me to stroke one off. "Hard." Lifting her fingers, she made a heart. "Love hard, Salvatore."

And she got up and walked off into the kitchen completely buck ass naked. The door was cracked, and I spotted Trudy in her black bra.

Good Lord, what are we doing?

I didn't know if she was coming back or if I was supposed to await my death or what. I envisioned Navarro coming into the room, roughing me up, and burying my ass in a mess of canned greens all because I couldn't shoot my fucking load.

Angela returned with two cold beers and a cup of ice water. I don't know if I've ever slammed back beer quite that fast. It was amazing. I watched her pour the contents of the cup into the basin as I mentally prepared for the extreme shift. I quietly suspected Navarro was into torture, and this was just the cusp of his proverbial iceberg.

Remember when I said everything with Trudy Diaz played into the future. It was true. Angela reported to Navarro. And Navarro reported to his one man.
And I passed her climate change with remarkable ease.

She ended up riding my cock until almost dawn. I came once when the pink of the sun started cresting over the horizon, but Angela had a damn good time all night long. I slept for a few hours and woke with a chill on the soaked bed.

I glanced around the room in a daze.

She was gone.

My body ached as I lifted onto my feet and opened the door stark ass naked. Everything was gone—the pots, pans, dishes, and the people. I found Trudy on a pew. She was covered by a tapestry throw embellished with an Ecuadorian flag.

"Trudy…" I whispered, gently shaking her leg and praying to fuck she wasn't dead. Her eyes opened. "Where did they go?"

"They're umbra," she replied, sitting up as I

plopped onto the pew at her feet. She was topless. "They come. And they go. Check the altar. You'll find coffee and leftovers."

"Did you…"

"I was feeling a bit spry after our inspirational romp," she confided with a smirk. "And I might have entertained Navarro and his right-hand guy, Chavez."

Running my fingers into my curls, I bent over and stared at the floor. "Jesus fuck, what did you get me into."

"Look at it this way, you can deal with the Latinos, or you can deal with the Irish."

I leaned back and rolled my eyes. "You're asking if I want roasted guinea pig or black pudding…"

"Essentially." She sympathetically smiled. "Trust me. You are far better off starting with Navarro than any leprechaun. That shit about four-leaf clovers and gold pots at the end of the rainbow ain't nothing but a load of horse shit to get you to turn your back to them. They'll stab you first and ream your ass out second. With Latinos, you get the privilege of a beer and a lay before they kill you."

"Oh, Jesus… This isn't happening."

"Yes, it is," she reaffirmed, rubbing my back. "The ball is in motion, and we have to act quickly."

"Angela was…"

"Oh, I know all about Angela." She smiled, scouting over the altar. "Not because she and I…but because she is…very good at what she does. Go get the coffee," she soothed. "We'll get dressed and go home."

"Did you tell them where we were yesterday?"

"Not directly," she said as I stood. "Emiliano is very good at narrowing in on what he wants."

"You?"

"No, honey…*you*."

6

HOLD MY HAND

We arrived back at her house by seven o'clock on Sunday. Despite driving and thinking of how to thank her for the weekend, the words just wouldn't come. Trudy came to mean so much to me in such a short expanse of time that my brain couldn't catch up to even begin to process it all.

"I guess I should be going," I mentioned, stepping out of the truck. "It was…*interesting*."

"Why don't you stay for dinner?"

"I can," I replied, lifting my phone. "But I have midnight mass."

Her brow furrowed. "Father Quinn?"

"He resides at the address."

She bit her lip and stared at the screen. "Salvatore…"

"Say it."

"You need to be careful," she urged with desperation. "Let me feed you before you go deal with that."

"Do you know anything about him?"

Pulling off her glasses, she snapped her teeth on the arm and blinked up several times. "I'm a Jew."

I smirked. "… And your point?"

"Ask me about the Catskills in the summer, but don't ask me about Mass," she snarked. "I'll tell you who you should talk to is my son."

"Is he Catholic?"

"Not exactly," she said, latching her arm into mine as we walked inside the house. "But his father is a devout…sinner."

"So, Saint is a sinner?"

"Pretty much." She sat her purse down in the kitchen and grabbed the bottle of whiskey. "But Deacon is very…I don't know how to define it…" She pulled out two glasses and started pouring the amber liquid as I sat in her nook. "He is very spiritual with gentle persuasion."

"Did he have a bar mitzvah?"

She snorted and slugged back the contents of her cup as she sat mine on the table. "Are you kidding? Javi would never hear of it."

"Is Javi Catholic?"

Pivoting on her heels, she went to grab the bottle of whiskey and returned to the table. Her hands trembled as she pulled out a smoke. I lit it, and then I poured her another glass of whiskey. "Javi is a faithful follower of one—Javi. He believes he's got the Father, the Son, and the Holy Ghost wrapped up in one belligerent package. Hell, he probably believes he's the Virgin Mary too." She leaned back and took a breath. "I just think if you are going to be crossing that line, then you best be on your A-fucking-game, much like you were at Navarro's table."

"I have to go," I mumbled, swirling the booze. "I can't get out of it."

"How did you get into it?"

"It was in the contract Jack Kerris brought me." I slipped and shut my eyes, praying she could keep her lips locked tight. "Fuck…"

"Jack?" Her maternal scowl looked like she was ready to rip the throat out of someone. "Jack? Anna got Jack to deliver the goods? Really? Why?"

I slumped back in the chair and spread my legs out. "You know, I don't know shit. He showed up, and I signed."

"No…no…you did fine," she said, puffing on the smoke. "I just don't understand the motivation behind it unless she was trying to get him on your radar. He's a slippery one. Did he insist on the meeting with Father Quinn?"

"Ya, said he had a client looking for a young man. I told him I don't fuck dudes. He promised there would be no sex. I challenged the rate and got more because he was male."

"Good for you." She stubbed her cigarette out and rested her tongue on her top teeth as she considered what to say. "I'm not going to tell you not to go. I'm going to tell you to be very careful because things get so lubed up at that level amongst the Kings and Gods that you won't ever get a grasp. You'll lose your footing fast and everything you earned this weekend at the church will be nothing more than a memory." She paused as I stroked my chin. "Do you want anything before you go?"

"Another blow job."

She cracked a smile. "You can call me anytime."

"Is your phone safe?"

"Ya, Javi doesn't give a flying fuck what I do any more as long as Deacon stays away from Delirium."

"Did Deacon do anything that wrong?"

"According to Javi, being a queer faggot was plenty enough sin from my bastard son."

I shook my head. "Why do you stay?"

"Because Javi is a stupid fuck worth millions, and

when you were raised in a tiny one-bedroom apartment in the Bronx, you don't forget."

"You're staying to get the money for Deacon?"

She grinned and pointed. "Bingo!"

"Does Javi have kids?"

"They're all estranged and want nothing to do with him," she said, squeezing my hand. "Eventually, he is going to piss the wrong SOB off, and kapow, Ma is worth a decent chunk of change."

"Does Deacon know what you're doing?"

"He does now," she softly answered. "He didn't understand when he was a child, and his ma was catching the blows."

"Does Javi still hit you?"

"Not since I came back from Mexico. At least, nothing serious enough to mention, an arm grab here and a quibble there."

I sighed because I understood way too well. "Don't let him hurt you."

"I won't."

I looked her straight in the eye. "If I find out he's hurting you, I will kill him."

She veered back, clearly unaccustomed to having someone defend her. "You do not get your hands dirty."

"I won't have a choice."

She polished off her drink, stood up, and walked to my side of the table. "I appreciate the generous offer, but I need you whole more than I want Javi dead."

Her legs straddled over mine, and I pulled her to sit on me. "I won't tolerate those I love being harmed, hurt, or abused. Do you understand me?"

The tension rose between us as I wrapped my arm around her bottom, and she pressed her hot core onto my thigh. I needed inside of her so I could forget what I was about to do. The power plays of the fetish were damned addictive, and I never once considered that she might reject or dismiss my notions because of my youth. She just wanted sex, but I craved the indescribable drug of obedience.

"I will be good to you, Sal." Her fingers brushed over my stubbled cheeks. "And for you."

"Get up and drop your jeans."

"Yes, Sir." She rapidly kicked her boots off and slinked out of the denim. Hungrily she licked her lips as I stared at the black panties with golden thread.

"Did you fuck Navarro?"

"Nah," she said. "We had a good time, but he isn't much for the act of sex." My brows lined as I gave her a questioning glance. "He would rather have his dick sucked than fucked. His…mother … he's fucked up, Raniero."

"… His mother molested him?"

"You could call it that, but it makes it sound far too blasé. She raped him for years, got pregnant with his child, and he ran off to join the military."

"Fuck…where is his child…now?"

"Not a clue, but this was years ago," she thoughtfully informed. "I had just started seeing Saint, so around 86 or 87. We started our affair, and it wasn't long before I was pregnant with Deacon."

"Is she dead?"

"Not that I know, but I'm not privy to everything involving Emiliano Navarro, for all I know, he had his son removed from the situation to avoid repeating the cycle."

"Name?"

Her eyes widened as she shook her head. "Not a fucking clue."

"I need to find your daughter and the status of his son."

"Only if you are ready to open up a big can of worms," she warned. "He guards his secrets like a vault of gold, but as I said, he does not have intercourse—*ever*."

"Ever?"

"Never," she reasserted. "It is a hard limit and not up for discussion with him. Don't bring it up, or you might not make it out alive."

"Jesus." I twirled my finger, and she spun around. "Can I be honest with you?"

"I would hope you feel like you can always be honest with me."

"And I'm not blowing smoke by saying this, but you have an incredible ass."

She grinned ear to ear. "I wish I could say it was because I worked for it, but I inherited it from my mother."

"Where was she from?"

"New York, but her parents were from Copenhagen."

"Danes, really?"

She nodded. "And my father was born in Portugal. Deacon resembles the Cruz line, who supposedly run back to the Visigoths."

"Shit," I marveled. "Goths…before it was hip."

She smiled. "Ya, Saint Cruz has some serious history. The blue eyes and blonde hair are from both sides, but he is much lighter than either of my parents. In the summer, it looks like golden threads."

"Like your panties…"

"Nice connection." She winked and smiled as I caught on. "Take care of my boy, Raniero."

"If your boy finds out what I'm about to do to his ma," I muttered, standing. "He isn't going to want me to take care of him because he will want to kill me."

"Then we make it so he can't…"

"Do your manipulations know no end?" I asked, bending her over the kitchen table and rubbing her ass.

She tossed her hair over her shoulder and glanced back to me. "All things in the interest of Deacon Cruz."

"You're a real bitch, ain't you?"

"For the right fucker, I'll be a slut, too."

I gripped her hair in my fist, grinding my erection against her rear. "Do you feel what you do to me?"

"Yes." Her eyes closed as she rocked her hips against the denim. I yanked the thin fabric from her flesh before squatting down. I bit her ass hard enough to leave marks, and she moaned. Slithering my finger between her thighs, I ran the pad along her slit and plunged deep into her wetness. "Fuck me, Sir."

"When am I going to see you again?"

"Next weekend?"

Pressing my nose to her skin, I threatened, "I should make you wait until then."

"You like punishing yourself?"

"I can be very well disciplined."

"You can be infuriating," she giggled as I shot up and smacked her ass hard with my hand. I quickly released my zipper and thrust my cock inside of her as my fingers twisted into her hair. "Shit...I knew you had it in you."

I tugged her hair back and growled low in her ear. "You have no idea what I am capable of..."

"I don't care! Just fuck me hard!"

I rolled my hips with a determination as I sought shelter from the impending storms of Sunday evening. I didn't want to play whipping boy for the priest, but feasting on Trudy would blunt the trauma.

I could get out of my head and remember this moment and how good she felt on my dick. I could play a mental game with myself, much like thinking about tits at the dentist's office, or being at the fetish club at sixteen when my father was using me as a punching bag. None of it was safe, but it worked.

. . .

The strange part of using visualization is I still do it today. I honed the skill over the years because I had to in order to survive. There is no way I would be alive if I hadn't figured it out early on. And it is a dangerous deception slowly cannibalizing my sanity.

"Sally," she moaned beneath me. "Take it, please…"

I knew what she wanted—a rough ride to feel in the morning. She needed the ache, the slow torturing reminder of what a man could do to her body. It was fucked up.

And so was I.

My hand braced on her hip as I fucked her without any regard. She wanted to be used and abused, and I needed to fucking do it. "Do you like it when I fuck you?"

"I like your dick way more than I should."

"I'm a demanding ass, Trudy," I professed, loosening my grip in her hair and trailing my fingertips around her neck.

"I don't give a damn as long as you're good."

"Don't fuck me over, bitch."

"I won't," she whispered, falling prey to my touch. "Ever."

With my heart racing, I pushed her down hard against the table and backhanded her ass. "I ought to whip you with my belt for that stunt this weekend. Did you suck their dicks like a good little whore? Did you swallow all of their cum?"

"No," she cried out. "I let them come on my tits."

Fuck. Me.

I rammed into her with all I had, thrashing and thrusting, fighting against the bounds of a moral compass which ceased to exist in her presence. I knew better than to be fucking Deacon's Ma because I had an inkling our paths would eventually cross, and I would have to pay the piper. I would have to pay for these sins in her house.

But she was so good, so compliant.

So willing for my aching Dominant.

As time would prove, the unlimited subservience was a familial trait, and I was a goddamned fiend, pushing the boundaries and provoking the intimacy.

How far could we go?

Where would we end?

No one knew.

I do not advocate my methods. I'm telling you because you must not make the same mistakes. We fought and fucked, sometimes in the same breath. We hurt one another. We healed one another.

Without rules, I was a risky motherfucker as her words—if I got them, I don't know them—defined every course of action I took as a man, a Master, and a monster. There were no easy scenes with idle orgasms. My submissives ramped up the game, and I accepted the challenge.

We were born on the edge, skating on the sharpness of the blade.

And we didn't care about the cuts because we were meant to bleed.

But not everyone cares that much…not everyone likes pain that much.

I had a masochistic streak a mile wide running parallel alongside deviant sadism.

I was sweating again as I pumped into Trudy. I didn't wrap the package with her because she was my one, and I had eons of faith that she wouldn't be hooking up with random callers because there was only one me.

Ma was many things, but easy to spread was not one of them. I counted her lovers on the trip back home as she confessed her past.

Three husbands.

Six lovers.

I stopped moving, stilling inside of her drenched pussy. "Who was your first husband, Trudy?"

"... Does it matter?"

"Yes," I replied, stepping back and pulling out as she slowly turned and propped against the table. "Who was your first husband?"

"Carlo Torrente."

"The New York mob boss?"

"The one and only," she replied, easing her bottom onto the table and lighting a smoke. "We met by accident. I was fifteen and he was twenty-one. After three years of sneaking out and late-night meetings, we eloped, and our parents found out."

"Oh my God…"

"My family was mad I married a Catholic, his family threatened to disown him for marrying a Jew, and the marriage was annulled after four days. You have to understand that back then, these things mattered to our parents."

"I'm sorry," I mumbled, feeling guilty for pushing for her answer. "Really sorry."

"Carlo knew Anna, and he encouraged me to visit. I packed one suitcase, kissed my parents goodnight, and disappeared in the night on a bus bound for Texas. I never went back home."

"You loved him…"

"I did," she whispered, shrugging. "I still do. I always will. That is why I won't get involved with Delarte, no matter how much money or what gifts he sends. I don't want to be in that kind of love again. I married my second husband in a rebound move, ended up getting knocked around, and knocked up. I knew Javi because they were in the same club. I called him, got an abortion, and left Ricky Slater."

"What happened to him?"

"He died in 1987," she vacantly said. "Freakish… car explosion…in the middle of the Louisiana backwoods…"

"Saint killed him."

"He wants to kill Javi too, but he understands the challenges," she elaborated, clasping her hands together as tears filled her eyes. "I love Saint a lot, but he won't leave Marlena because of their fucking idiotic daughter, Wendy. I was just his mistress."

"And what about your other lover?"

"Javi was convinced I was sleeping with "Crazy" Humphrey Robbins. Guns went off, five-year-old Mary Elizabeth Conmeyer took the fatal shot, and my son was baptized in her blood."

"You weren't sleeping with "Crazy" Humphrey…"

"No, I hadn't cheated on Javi yet…but I did with Mary Elizabeth's dad, Caruth. I could make him feel something when he felt nothing but bitter sadness."

"Where is he?"

She sighed with remorse. "Why are we doing this right now?"

"Because I need to know how many loose strings you have blowing in the wind that could whip back like barb wire and rip us to shreds."

"Caruth passed away after being shot in Godland."

"Who shot him?"

Lost in the memory, she shook her head. "He called it friendly fire."

"Javier Diaz."

"You got it."

I tugged my jeans up, leaving them undone and loose on my hips. "The statistical odds of me making it out alive by agreeing to hook up with you are diminishing quick."

"Carlo won't touch you."

"Thank God for small favors, but he is in New York."

"Saint is quickly losing interest in me because he's got his eyes set on some new young thing, Amber Rosen. She's a stripper at Gina's bar, goes by Mae East. Are you going to remember all of this?"

I paced back and forth across the length of her kitchen. "Every fucking word."

"Javi is…into the sheep." I furrowed a brow. "Young club sluts. Stumped you with that one."

"I never claimed to be a biker."

"Thank God for small favors." She winked as her mascara trickled over her cheek.

I stopped in the center of the kitchen. "Who was your third lover?"

"Just some guy I met in New Orleans."

"When?"

"A few years ago, when Saint started banging the pole humper. He was in Gina's, and I nodded, and he followed."

I grabbed a smoke off the table and asked, "Is it still going on?"

She hesitated too long. "He's a Dominant. We aren't exactly lovers in a traditional sense."

"You paid him?"

"I paid him," she confirmed, nodding. "But, we only met four times."

"And where is Deacon?"

She uncontrollably rocked. "I asked him to help me out with my boy."

"You sent your son to a fucking Master?"

"I sent my son to be saved."

"Jesus, lady!" Walking away, I gripped the bridge of my nose. "I get we're not innocent, but you sent your possibly gay son to a Master in New Orleans."

"I did."

"A kid you know has gulped down buckets of squiz," I angrily hissed as she came barreling towards me. Her hand impacted my cheek with such force I could've sworn she was a nun. "He isn't going to survive that."

"You go to church and tell me that, Sal," she snapped. "You aren't innocent, so stop acting like it! You talk about the wire whipping us to smithereens, but you've got some skeletons! Don't act like you aren't guilty!" She turned away, but came back for more with a point of her finger. "And don't you ever talk about Deacon like that again! He's a good boy. A nice boy. I had him arrested to save him because he's a better fucking person than either of us will ever be! Do you hear me?"

"You what?" I bellowed, rubbing my cheek. I was certain she left a handprint. I cracked my knuckles, furious at the circumstances spinning wildly out of control. "What am I supposed to do at church?"

"Get down on your knees and pray because sometimes," she whispered, sobbing. "Sometimes, you have to play the fucking game." She grabbed her clothes and stomped towards her bedroom. She yelled over the railing, *"Sometimes, you have to fucking trust people!"*

"People lie!"

"And sometimes you have to take the risk! Just like you did with Nicky in coming to Texas. Hell, just like you did by signing that fucking contract!"

"That contract is the *only* reason I'm still here."

"If you believe that...if you *truly* believe that... you've got a lot to learn."

Her door slammed.

And I walked out.

7

HELP ME

"What happened? And what do you mean you had a fight?"

On the speakerphone, Charlotte drilled through twenty questions as I raced down the backroads towards Sugargrove. Nothing like an overly hyper teenage girl to conduct a thorough interrogation.

"I'm pretty sure I fucked up big time."

"Nah, I don't think that's possible."

I told her everything, from the bathtub encounter to Navarro's sister. Again, if I ended up face down in the dirt, someone needed to know what all the fuck was going on. I didn't know if it was one-hundred percent safe to be confiding in Charlotte because of who I was. I could be putting her in jeopardy, but she was the one person my age who seemed to get it. All of it. From the utter insanity of being new in Sugargrove to being a fumbling eighteen-year-old, she understood me. Because at the end of the day, I was still just a kid who was faking it until I made it.

"Are you going to see Father Quinn?"

"I have to."

"Are you okay?"

The truth was, I didn't know. I was hurt, pissed, sad…and a thousand other emotions. I didn't want to lose Trudy, but damn she could push my buttons.

Maybe that was the point.

"I'll be fine. I just fucked up is all."

"You didn't fuck up."

"Have you met Trudy Diaz?"

She giggled. "I've lived in Sugargrove for almost sixteen years. I know everyone. I played with her little boy when I was five at Quad-F. We lit sparklers, ate hot dogs, and he gave me a piggyback ride under the fireworks."

"That little boy is twenty now," I snarked, realizing what all she said. "And since when is Quad-F family-friendly?"

"It has never been, and that's why Anna kept a bunch of us kids at her house. And I get Deacon's an adult now, dumbass," she teased. "But Trudy is good people, Sal. If she bit, then it was for a good reason."

"Just so you know, I hate it when you're right."

"What are you going to do?"

Turning into the church parking lot, I replied, "Ask the Padre if I can confess my sins and send Trudy a dozen pink roses tomorrow morning?"

"It's a start," she said with a sigh. "Have a good night. Be safe. And text me when you get back home."

"Hey," I mumbled, putting the car in park. The lot was completely dark except for one light deep in the woods next to the rectory. "Love you, babe."

"I know," she happily giggled. "Love you more."

I stepped out of the car, ran my fingers through my hair, and pulled my ball cap on. It was a safety net—a crutch and comfort. I grabbed my hoodie even though it was still well over 85°F, lit a smoke, and ambled through the parking lot to my demise. I might as well have been walking the plank into perilous, capsizing seas, threatening to swallow me whole.

I wasn't nervous because he was a priest.

I was fucking terrified because he was a man.

And I did not get along with men.

Piano music filled the weighted night air pregnant with moisture as I passed by the cathedral and then the small house with the back deck where Perrine served me up lemonade and love. I took one step up and spotted a man in a sport coat. With slicked-back raven hair, chiseled angles crafted by the heavens, and deep-set, foreboding eyes, he looked like a damn model or a movie star. He was simply stunning.

And not a priest.

"Excuse me. I was supposed to meet Father Quinn."

Standing up, he smirked and extended his hand. "Boston. Come sit down and have a chat with me."

"Who are *you*?"

"Your savior."

The glow of several citronella candles flickered as he poured two glasses of whiskey. Jim Beam. The amber tranquility glowed in the light of the flames. The setting was mysteriously magical and matched by the enigmatic stud extending his hand. "I'm Salvatore Raniero, and I'm supposed to be meeting…"

"Me," he interrupted with a passive simper. "But I couldn't very well call you up and tell you to come to meet me. You never would've agreed to that lunacy."

"Right," I replied, nodding at the peculiarity of the situation and tensing every muscle in my body. "Because I don't entertain men. Now, if you'll excuse me, I'm going to find Father Quinn." I moved away, refusing his handshake.

"He isn't here," he informed with a commanding tone as I turned back to face him. "Why don't you sit down and have a chat with me, Boston?"

"I don't know who you are," I replied, heading for the steps. "And I have no desire to talk to you."

"You want to talk about the busted lip and broken bones and...*Bilal*?"

Caught in his trap, I stopped dead in my tracks and exclaimed, "Who the fuck are you?"

"Sit. Down. Now. Lucas." His voice boomed with authority as my heart rattled inside of the cage. No one in Sugargrove knew about my past, especially concerning my best friend, Bilal. I took a seat in the wicker chair as his perfect fingers handed a glass to me. *He knew. They knew. My gig was up.* With an even tempo, he clasped his fingers together, and politely said, "Please, if you will."

"I shouldn't be here," I muttered, fearing the worst. I was a dumb kid who got wrapped up in something horrible. I lowered my head in shame. "Shit…"

"This meeting never occurred," he said, expanding his arms. "You do not know me, and I do not know you."

Giving a side-eyed glance to him, I shook my head. "I'm not supposed to know Jack Kerris, either."

"That is correct," he acknowledged, picking up the box of Camels. Lighting a smoke, he exhaled a nicotine cloud above his head. His bold, yet understated, confidence was out of this world. "But this is going to come down to one thing."

"What's that?"

"Who you trust more," he contended, handing the cigarette to me. He lit another for himself. "I know who is watching you and why. I can assist you in navigating through these murky waters if you'll allow me to."

Taking a long drag on the smoke, I questioned, "What do you want?"

"More than anything to give you *freedom*."

"Whatever you're offering, I'm not buying," I rallied, fighting for absolution to past sins. Trudy nailed it. I had a closet overflowing with bones from the dearly departed. I didn't just set off on a track away from my father and family but myself. And now, it seemed, those vigilant ghosts were haunting me from the grave. With my thug on parade, I challenged, "And I'm not sucking your dick if you ask me to."

He chuckled. "Don't fret. I won't ask." A brief flirtatious smirk lifted on his lips like he was the son of Satan himself. And the worst part was—*he was so damned gorgeous*. With a twinkle in his eyes, he declared, *"I'll* tell you when to suck my cock, and you will."

The humid air clung heavy as a light fog clustered around the trees. Starting to sweat, I pulled off my hoodie, and his penetrating eyes never once left me. He was gawking, blatantly staring, and a sense of unease lingered in my breath. I didn't know this guy as dampness welled in my eyes. "Why do you keep looking at me?"

"Because I'm imagining how beautiful all that taut olive skin will be when you're naked and tangled in my sheets."

"I told you," I repeated, trying to hold my stance and losing ground fast. I gulped back the whiskey. "I don't do men," I snipped. "Thank you for the drink, stranger. I'm leaving. Goodnight."

"If you get up, there will be consequences for your actions."

"… You're going to punish me?"

"Oh, yes, Boston," he salaciously muttered. "I'm going to punish you for many, many nights to come."

I vacated the chair, turning my back, and he was on me in seconds. Pinning my arm back, he pushed my torso against the back wall of the rectory. My hat fell off in the skirmish. "I told you to play nice, Sally boy."

My lip trembled with fear at his strength. He wasn't big or bulky, but his moves were sharp and quick. I was not going to live because I had fucked up royally and this was the end. "Are you going to kill me?"

"No," he whispered against my ear as he rubbed his arousal against my hip. "You can make this easy, or you can make this hard."

"Feels like I already made something hard."

Instantly, his free hand grabbed my cock, and I gasped, closing my eyes. He was winning the round, the fight, and me. His illicit groping was *sweet*.

Taboo. Dirty. Claiming.

"And I'm not the only one," he insisted, raising his hand up my shirt. He trailed his palm over my belly and landed on my heart. I calmed, slowing my breaths. "Now sit your pretty ass down in that chair and let's talk."

"Tell me your name," I begged, knowing I couldn't get out of it. He was fiercely mean and beautifully hot. My eyes filled with tears as I met his gaze and muttered, "Please, Sir."

Beneath the gold embellished wrought-iron gas lamps, he spun my body, keeping my shoulders pinned to the wall, and slowly swerved closer.

Was he smelling me?

His moss-colored eyes blinked up as he breathed upon my lip. He smelled like whiskey and cigarettes, and *home*. He lightly nipped my bottom lip, and I closed my eyes as he gently kissed me like he owned me.

Because he did.

"You can call me Master," he oozed with intimidation. "Or, you can call me Dominic Gennaro."

My blood pressure spiked as I choked for air and mentally tumbled into an epic level meltdown. I was seized by his carriage and decimated by the truth. "Chicago mafia. Rivals. My father hates you."

"And I hate your father. But more precisely, your father hates my father, Angelo Gennaro. As their sons, I'd like to come to an agreement."

"What do you mean?"

"Work with me," he eagerly proposed.

"I'm already working with Trudy." And then it hit me. "Fuck, you have Deacon."

He boisterously laughed. "Oh, I do have that which you covet, but don't make it sound like I have him held captive in a cage."

"I don't covet him."

"Don't lie," he warned, tightening his hold.

I tilted my head against the wall and sought in the escape of the beadboard ceiling. "She was in on it..."

His fingers grazed over my lips and neck and chest as he rhythmically called my bluff. "Anna, Perrine, Trudy, Navarro, and Father Quinn..." The pads of his fingers edged around the waist of my jeans. I was emphatically hard, desperate for more. And I hated myself for such. "We all worked to accommodate one mafia son."

"What about Jack?"

Now that he thoroughly had my attention, he released his grip on my shoulder. The worst part was I missed the guidance of his firm hand. "He's part of the equation we don't trust."

"You aren't the only one," I muttered, relaxing. "What do you want me to do?"

He mischievously grinned and strummed his

finger over my cheek. "What do I need you to do? Or what do I want you to do?"

With bated breath, I responded, "All of the above."

"Be my pet, Salvatore. Do everything I say. And I will make sure in the next ten years, you have everything you ever dreamed."

"… At what cost?" I balked.

"Do everything I say."

Shit—I must've missed that part because of the lack of blood flow.

"May I ask a question?"

"Of course, but I reserve the right not to answer," he replied, still touching my face. "I will always tell you the truth when I can."

I tilted my head in disbelief as if my hero had fallen from grace. "… You'd lie to me?"

"If it meant protecting you?" He was seriously stoic in his focus. "I'd lie... I'd kill... I'd die."

My expression contorted. "Why?"

"What is your question?" he asked segueing.

My tongue zipped over my lips as I struggled to say the words. "How did you know about Bilal?"

"We've had Nick Cristos watching you for years."

"Shit." My eyes closed as I bounced my head against the wood. "Fuck!"

"But tell me, why would such a freely loving boy such as yourself find pay dirt here in Texas and be so vehement against handling male clients?"

My jaw stiffened as a single tear spilled down my cheek. "Because I didn't want another broken hand from getting caught stroking one off on my secret crush."

"How many times did he do that?" Silence filled my voice as I couldn't muster up the courage to answer. "Where is Bilal, Sal?"

The heartache poured like a waterfall from my eyes. "He's dead."

"And how did he die?"

"My father yanked his body out of the trunk on the bridge and threw him in the river when I was thirteen because I wouldn't leave him alone, and breaking my fucking hands wasn't working anymore. He killed him." I collapsed in his warm arms as his fingers brushed through my curls.

"You heard his screams and blamed yourself."

"He went missing," I whimpered, slobbering on his dress shirt. "Nicky knew what was going on? And he didn't try and stop it?"

"Nick called, and we sent Delarte Cristos in, to try and reason with him. We failed you, not the other way around, son. You were a kid. This one isn't on you."

"I should've said something…"

"And what would that have gotten? You killed? Your mama with another black eye?"

I didn't know. There wasn't a right answer. "He was my best friend, and we were just messing around."

"But the undeniable hunger was there, and you felt it again when you saw the photos of Deacon."

I was out of options. There was no use in denial because Dom knew every-*fucking*-thing about me. "I need someone able to handle my bullshit."

"What do you think I'm offering?"

I gripped his arms as I bawled, heaving, and sobbing. I never told anyone the truth, but Dom became my savior, riding a white horse on a very tenebrous night. And his enemy blood infiltrated my veins, and we became kindred. He was my new family…my new home…my only salvation…and the only absolution I needed. He was a Gennaro; I was a Raniero. And there was no reason this should've ever happened.

"I don't know. What are you going to do?"

"I'm taking you to the top of the game, but in the

end, I get the kill shot. You don't need his blood on your hands. It's mine."

With wide eyes, I pressed my greedy lips to his, seeking what I had been ashamed of for so long. He didn't allow my apologies or excuses but welcomed my resilient hesitations. I couldn't stop the crave and kept searching for the spark. I hated myself for so long, feeling the way I did about girls and boys, that when I finally reached his shores, I basked in all my glory. And I handed over my soul to a stranger in the darkness.

His intoxicating kiss sent waves of pleasure through my body. He parted from my lips, tugging my shirt off, and tossing his sport coat onto a chair. His mouth returned to mine, trailing down to my neck, and over my heart. He slowly lowered to his knees—*my Dominant*—and meticulously undid my belt and jeans. His eyes blinked up to mine. "You must never tell anyone of our training."

With his face mere inches from my cock, I conceded, "I will never tell anyone, Master."

The first flick of his tongue against my shaft was pure bliss. His mouth broke the barriers of my virginity with men, and it was splendor. I tumbled into an absolute nirvana with every stroke of his lips.

He paused, holding my dick in his warm palm and admired, "You're beautiful, Boston."

I didn't ask how often I'd be seeing him. Judging our connection, I understood his shadowy presence would appear regularly at the cathedral for practice rounds of his tutelage. "May I touch you, Sir?"

"Yes," he muttered, licking the head of me. "I am yours."

My fingers eased through his long dark hair, messing his slicked-back style up. The pads of my fingers felt the stubble on his cheeks. I lifted my fingers, bringing them to my nose. "You smell like one hell of a man."

He stopped sucking and chuckled. "I am a hell of a man about to take you on the journey of your life."

"What about the priest?"

"You will meet with him every Wednesday after mass," he instructed, maintaining a constant pulse on my cock. "And he will not be touching you as I do. His only need is in your masochism. He is a sadist with certain preferences to crops and whips."

"I take his lashings…"

With a smirk, he interrupted, "And you wait for my arrival Thursday before your weekends with clients."

I snickered, "Not going to let them have that joy?"

"Not a fucking chance in hell," he replied, running his tongue the length of me. "And you will be chaste from the priest's punishments until my visits."

"Shit." I leaned my head against the wall.

"Discipline, Boston."

"Yes, Sir."

Removing his hand from my cock, he slowly stood, and I noted his wobble. "Two prosthetics."

"… Military?"

"Former, but I lost them in a motorcycle accident," he remorsefully said. "It's all good. Trust me. You'll learn to fear the days I show up with a cane in my hand."

My mouth watered at the thought as a shiver went through my spine. "Are you married?"

"No."

"Involved with anyone?"

"You," he immediately answered. "You are my only goal until I get you self-sustaining, at which point, we will modify our arrangement." He scanned over my physique with a ravenous gaze. "Damn, I didn't expect you to be quite so…*incredible*. Take your clothes off and lean over the rail." He said the words easily like he was asking me to fetch his drink. I gawked, stunned and unsure. "Now, Raniero."

"Yes, Master." I kicked off my shoes and dropped my jeans. I giggled.

His eyes shone with a proudness as he crossed his arms. "Something funny?"

"I'm wearing Deacon's boxers."

"You haven't worn underwear in years." He winked. "Nick is highly astute with a keen sense of awareness and attention to detail."

"I'm quite knowledgeable of Nicky's *habits*," I replied, stepping out of my jeans and cautiously stepping towards the rail. I glanced over my shoulder and asked, "Are you training Deacon too?"

"In a different way," he informed, pulling something from his pocket. "More complimentary to your high energy. Before you ask, I am not doing with Cruz what I am about to do to you, but he is definitely of equal beauty."

White knuckling the rail, I mumbled, "He's perfection."

Tucking his hand between my cheeks, he carefully lubed my ass. I flinched, realizing this was *seriously* about to occur. It was one thing to smack my meat thinking about it and an entirely different beast *actually* doing it. "You're okay," he reassured. "Breathe."

"I'm scared…"

"Of what?"

"Liking it too much," I admitted, staring at the trees. Dom was so precise and methodical. Every move was calculated and calibrated to whittle away at my nerves. He enjoyed the mind fuck as I waited on the precipice of my rebirth. "And what happens…"

"I don't know." Gripping my hip, he snorted as the sound of his zipper dropping resonated through every pore of my being. "I will not even begin to speculate what will happen when you two meet. You may kill one another. You may not like each other. Or you may find exactly what you've been looking for, but what I do know is your lips must stay sealed. If anyone discovers the Raniero son is kneeling for the Gennaro son, all hell will break loose. Do not speak about it with anyone, even those involved. Anna does not need to know the extent of our affair. And neither does Charlotte."

Lowering my head, I locked my fingers together and remembered all the times I heard the bones snap at the hands of my father. I fought back the screams of horror from Bilal and recalled the irreverent laughter and smiles as we grew from innocence to something more. I wanted him. I loved him. And he wouldn't have been happy with my vehement denial and guilt. He would want me to do this. He would want this because this was who I should've become had my trajectory not been knocked down repeatedly by a monster. "Do it, please, Sir."

His thrust came on rapid, in an instant, impaling his shaft to the hilt inside of my ass, and he stilled, waiting and allowing my breath to return to normal. "It will get better," he encouraged. "You will loosen and enjoy it. Take your time, Salvatore. Take your time."

With my mouth hanging wide open and my eyes shut tight, I gently moved, feeling the thickness of his cock and every ripple therein. "Holy fuck…"

"You could say that."

I laughed, easing the tension in my body and rocked against him. He didn't demand my moves or command the attention but focused his light on my future as he fought alongside me. "You feel good."

"It was never supposed to feel bad." We weren't talking about the physical distinctions, but the emotional hurdles as our fluidity sprouted with intimacy. "Trust me to care for you." His hand lassoed around my dick as we moved in unison that hot

Texas night. "I will hurt you when the time is right, and you're in a more stable place."

"I hope so, Sir. I hope."

This was about his serving my needs, not the other way around.

In the truest sense, I was never Dom's submissive, nor did he ever demand such of me. I was a Master in the making, and he was my finest teacher. His adept brilliance proved my sacrifices worth it.

I will forever be a masochist as pain ignites my growth. Eventually, the expanse of my physical language yearned for greater exploration, inciting my sadistic endeavors.

With Dom, everything from my mafia business to accepting my bisexuality could breathe and naturally evolve. He never pushed, fostering my incremental growth as it came.

He licked and cleaned my wounds, beginning the process of healing, and giving the most precious gift of his patience.

In exchange, I promised him the kill shot.

And boundless access to my rebellious dark prince.

I have never spoken about the depth of our initial relationship until now, but you should know long before my future wife brought him into my world, I knew Dom. And I knew him well.

. . .

"You asked why I would lie, kill, or die for you earlier," he whispered an hour later. He was smoking a joint as I laid my head on his thigh and he stroked my hair. "The answer is simple. Because you are me. And now, you are mine."

"Thank you, Daddy."

"You're very welcome, son."

CLIENT #2

The twists keep coming...

Sal Raniero's Little Black Book 2

"You're the one-night fantasy, Sal."

Every client reveals more truths.

Can I keep playing both sides or will the dirty games turn sinister?

On the terrace of the coffee shop Monday morning, I listened as Charlotte aimlessly gabbed on about her latest boyfriend. Finally, I put her on mental ignore and wondered if I would hear from my secret savior before our meeting Thursday.

Amidst the cups and salads, my phone buzzed on the table.

"One sec," I said to my overly hyper companion as I picked up the call. "Hello?"

"Sal, come out to the house tonight at seven." Her sensual voice intrigued my mind with her cool, sleek charm. "I'm texting you the address now. I cannot wait to meet you."

The line went dead as the message appeared.

Flinging my sunglasses off, I gawked at the name. "Charlotte, I have to go meet with your aunt."

With her expression turning sour, she gasped. "Oh, my God! That's so not fair!"

Ella Hemsworth.
    Rich. Intelligent. Hot as sin.
    And Charlotte's Aunt.
    Need I say more?

Printed in Great Britain
by Amazon